IN YOU, I EXIST

Kranthi Kumar

Disclaimer 1:

No part of this book may be reproduced, distributed, or transmitted in any form or by any means, including photocopying, recording, or other electronic or mechanical methods, without the prior written permission of the author, except in the case of brief quotations for reviews or academic purposes.

Disclaimer 2:

This is a work of fiction. Any resemblance to actual persons, living or dead, real events, religions, or beliefs is purely coincidental. The characters, events, and settings are products of the author's imagination and are not intended to represent or offend any individual, group, culture, or faith.

First Edition: March 2025
Published by: Kranthi kumar

CONTENTS

Am I getting older by chasing time, Or is

time getting older by chasing me?

Chapter 1
Memories

The sky hovered above him, soft clouds gliding by. He felt unsteady, starting to lose balance. His steps grew erratic, almost moving independently as the sky consumed his thoughts. He extended his arms, gazed upwards, and kept walking. The clouds morphed into new shapes each time he opened and shut his eyes. Suddenly, he halted when a thick branch from a tree blocked his view. Lowering his arms, he sought the branch's origin and spotted a tall tree about fifteen feet to his right.

"Hey, did you notice that? The clouds are changing so fast. Are they altering for themselves or for someone else? Look again; they're shifting. Isn't that fascinating?"

A soft breeze brushed against his back as he watched the clouds.

"Did you feel that? Maybe the wind that caressed me carried my thoughts into the sky and transformed them into clouds, forming new shapes. This suggests that those shifting forms embody my thoughts, indicating I am everywhere. Have you ever felt this way?"

He grinned at the tree.

"I feel for you, my friend. Don't you ever get tired of standing still all the time? Let me share something: movement is life; being motionless feels like being dead."

With another smile, he spread his arms, looked up at the sky, and resumed walking, observing the changing clouds. It seemed the clouds wanted the sun to see him, altering their shapes to reveal him to the light. Slowly, he closed his eyes.

Total Darkness…

He stood before his master, listening attentively.

"I am proud to have you as my student. You came here with a heavy heart and have gained so much knowledge. I hope this knowledge will someday evolve into wisdom. I've taught you everything I can. Now, it is time for you to embark on your journey and meet my master. You will also be a wonderful student for him. Go, my friend. Begin your journey and let it guide you to your goal."

Tears brimmed in his eyes as he gazed up at his master. These tears reflected the deep gratitude that every student holds for their teacher. For a master, this kind of appreciation is priceless. He bowed with respect, turned, and set off on his path. As he exited the spiritual school, he observed the river flowing alongside him.

"This river brought me here like a collection of broken stones, and my master has shaped me into who I am today. I am heading where my master wishes: to his master, the enlightened one, the only master of our time who has attained enlightenment. I hope my journey will lead me to the enlightened one's spiritual school. I hope one day, I will be his favourite student. I hope to discover myself in that spiritual school. I hope to find my ultimate bliss.”

He paused for a moment, standing still, filled with pride and joy. A smile spread across his face. Then, he slowly opened his eyes, looked up, and saw the sky. It was bright, and the clouds danced joyfully. He felt happiness as he recalled memories of his master; he had been his master’s favourite student. With these joyful memories, he began walking again beneath the vast sky, spreading his arms like a bird in flight.

“I am the luckiest woman to have someone like you as my husband. Every day feels like we got married just yesterday. Today, I want to share something with you that I believe will be the happiest news possible. But now you’re telling me that you’re leaving,” Mayuri, his wife, said with a heavy heart and deep sadness, tears streaming down her face.

“What did you want to share with me?” he asked.

"Now, what is the use of telling you about that?"

"Please don't say that, dear. I feel like I'm dying inside."

They both held each other's hands and cried.

"I can compel you to stay with me forever if I choose, but I cannot control your thoughts and desires." She gently touched his cheek, full of concern, and said, "How can you live without me, my love?"

When she said that, he started to cry like a child. Then, he took her hand, which felt heavy with the weight of his tears. She embraced him, and they both wept.

"Let us cry together for the last time, my love," she said without controlling her crying.

She felt that this moment was perfect for revealing what she wanted to say, as she could no longer tell by looking at his face.

"You're going to be a father; we will be parents," she said.

When she said that, he immediately tried to pull away from her hug to see her face.

However, she held him tightly, preventing him from breaking free from her embrace.

"Please let me see you now."

"No, my love, please, I can't bear to look into your eyes right now."

"Please don't kill me; I beg you, let me see you now."

They both came out of that hug, crying uncontrollably. Somehow, she managed to come back to normal. She had to because she didn't have any other option.

"Please don't cry. Look at me. From now on, you must take care of yourself. Begin your journey and reach your destination. I will take care of our love," she said as she placed his hand on her womb, smiling through her pain.

"Who is going to take care of you then?" When he asked that question, she couldn't hold back the pain within her.

"I have many memories of you; those are enough to take care of me till my last breath."

She withdrew her hands from him, and as she did, he realised he must begin his own journey without her. Silence enveloped them as they gazed at each other for a moment. She glanced at the pendant around his neck. Understanding, he removed the pendant and handed it to her. He looked at her one last time before turning away and walking off.

She quickly turned away, closed her eyes, and began to cry, pressing the pendant to her heart.

"If I could erase the steps I'm taking away from her, I would find happiness. Together, we would experience joy in our love. Today, she revealed that we would be parents, and in response, I said I was leaving, uncertain about when or if I would return. I felt regret for her choice of me as a partner. I no longer feel worthy of her love. Yet, I can't go back and stay with her forever. I don't want to die without understanding my purpose in life. I want eternal happiness. I want to know what happiness truly is. I need to understand who is abandoning my wife and walking alone now. I want to discover who I am. That is my goal.

As he continued walking away from her, his feet felt increasingly heavy with each stride. Every step seemed like a burden, as if he carried the weight of the world. It felt as though he was walking into complete darkness, with no light visible ahead.

Total Darkness…

Chapter 2

Anvesh

He opened his eyes, looked at the sky, and gradually lowered his hands, sensing the sorrow of the clouds wrapping around him as their mood shifted from joy to sadness. There was no sunlight on him. As he looked up at the sky, he saw that the sun was obscured by clouds. Feeling downcast, he turned to gaze at the tree he had just walked by.

"My name is Anvesh. It has been fifteen years since I left my wife. I have visited many spiritual institutions and gained significant knowledge from various teachers, yet none of their lessons have been able to erase the burden of memories I carry. However, I will not remain here forever like you. I will continue my journey as long as I encounter the enlightened one, and I am confident that I will discover who I am and what my purpose on this Earth is."

Feeling as though he were not a bird able to spread his wings, he walked heavily, weighed down by his memories.

After roughly four hours, he paused—not from exhaustion, but because he came across a fork in the road. Uncertain which way to go, he searched for someone to ask for directions but found no one. Eventually, he spotted a man resting under a tree. Anvesh approached him. As he drew closer, he noticed the man had one leg flat on the ground and the other bent, resting on top of it. Dressed in tattered black clothes, the man was a figure of desolation.

Anvesh halted in front of him and said, "Excuse me."

The man sat upright and replied, "What do you need to excuse yourself from?"

Anvesh looked at him; he appeared very ancient.

"I need to move forward, but I'm uncertain about which direction to choose," Anvesh expressed.

The old man said, "Listen, my young friend. You have two options. The first option is a familiar path that many have successfully taken to reach their destinations. You need not doubt that this path will lead you there; simply follow the footprints of those who travelled before you. Think of it as a sheep following its shepherd in a herd. The second option is an uncharted path; no one has returned to share their tale. If you choose this unknown route, you will need to forge your own way, which demands bravery and a readiness to explore your inner self. Please do not waste my time if you have already decided on the first path. If you're intrigued by the second, I will offer my guidance, but only once you choose to embark on that adventure."

Anvesh was immersed in deep thought.

The old man looked at him and realised that Anvesh was not in the position to make his own decisions at all. Then the old man leaned on the ground, closed his eyes, and covered his face with his torn cloth. Anvesh looked at him and realised that the old man wouldn't show any interest if he chose the first path. So, he selected the first path over the second one. He didn't want to take a risk further. Therefore, he chose an easy path. Instead of asking him further, he began his journey on the first path. He started to follow the footprints on that path. As he walked further, he experienced the weight on his shoulders increasing. That weight kept on increasing with each step he put forward. The surrounding darkness slowly consumed his path, causing him to become unaware of the outside world. All at once, the footprints vanished. The trail was entirely cloaked in darkness, and he could only hear his breath against the heavy burden.

Total darkness…

Chapter 3

Two Young Monks

Mokshith, a novice monk, lay on a rock, naturally flat, that resembled a bed, complete with a pillow. Beside him lay Dhruv, who was five years his senior. This naturally formed rock served as their resting spot. They weren't alone; a gentle stream meandered nearby, flowing into a pond where they could satisfy their thirst. Both wore long sky-blue garments, typical of monks, to cover their bodies. It was early morning when Dhruv awoke and looked at Mokshith, who was still fast asleep. His eyes fell on a copper glass situated between them, a vessel monks usually kept filled with water overnight. Quietly, Dhruv picked up the glass, careful not to wake Mokshith. He then poured water into Mokshith's ear, causing him to wake instantly, shouting Dhruv's name.

Dhruv then stood up and attempted to leave that place.

"Hey, hold on! This occurs to me repeatedly. Today, I promise you'll regret it."

"You, fool, first catch me if you can, then I'll listen to you," Dhruv said while running away from him.

Mokshith started to chase him through the forest. Dhruv kept running and made sure that Mokshith didn't catch him at all. Mokshith was trying very hard to catch him. After doing that for a while, Dhruv disappeared from Mokshith's sight. However, Mokshith didn't worry; knowing where Dhruv might be, he headed to the pond filled with lotus flowers where Dhruv was likely to be. He searched for Dhruv, but he was nowhere to be found. Mokshith began picking lotus flowers from the pond, which was one of his daily tasks. While gathering the flowers, he glanced into the water and noticed a reflection of something approaching from behind. It was Dhruv, coming up behind him. Before Mokshith could react, Dhruv pushed him into the water. Mokshith fell in, and Dhruv burst into laughter. Shortly after, Dhruv also jumped into the pond, and they splashed water on each other while playing together.

"Okay, stop. This time, you've won," said Mokshith.

"No, fool. I'll try again tomorrow. Tomorrow, I will push you once more," Dhruv declared.

"Who cares about tomorrow? Let's gather these flowers now," said Mokshith.

As Mokshith collected flowers, he observed the sun reflecting on the water next to the lotus he was about to pick.

As soon as he spotted the sun, he exclaimed, "Hey, Dhruv, he's arrived. I can go now." Mokshith hurriedly exited the pond, gripping a handful of lotus flowers.

As Mokshith ascended the hill, Dhruv called out, "Hey, don't leave me behind!"

"No, I won't wait; he's already waiting for me there."

Mokshith rushed along, and Dhruv smiled, already knowing where Mokshith was headed. They had engaged in the same activity daily since childhood. At 25, Dhruv is five years older than Mokshith, who is 20. Not a day went by without their meeting. Dhruv gathered a handful of lotus flowers, left the pond, and followed Mokshith's trail.

As Dhruv arrived at the hill's base, he looked up toward the peak, where Mokshith rested on a rounded stone. The hill was blanketed in vibrant green grass. From below, Dhruv could see Mokshith sitting on the rock, gazing at the sun, presenting a view of his back. The fabric Mokshtih wore fluttered in the wind and sparkled in the sunlight. Upon reaching the top, Dhruv discovered Mokshith serenely seated on the stone, enjoying the sun's warmth, with lotus flowers beside him.

Mokshith spotted Dhruv and remarked, "Look at him."

Dhruv came over, took a seat behind him, and admired the orange sun painting the sky in warm tones. He gently nudged Mokshith with his shoulder and inquired, "What message did he bring today?"

"I'm not sure. Whenever I see him, I feel like he's trying to convey something to me," Mokshith answered.

"What could that be?"

"I don't know. Maybe I need to be reborn every day, like him, to understand," Mokshith replied.

"Maybe you're not the right person to decipher his message."

"Then who is? Are you?"

"Yes, I am the one he wants to communicate with," Dhruv confirmed.

"So, why isn't he sharing anything with you?" Mokshith asked.

"I come here with you every day. If I were alone, he would share with me because he doesn't like your presence," Dhruv said, running away.

"How dare you say that? You fool, I'm going to get you now!" Mokshith shouted, chasing after Dhruv.

Mokshith and Dhruv sprinted down the hill, reaching the congregation just as it began. This grand event attracted thousands of students, many dressed in white — a privilege reserved for accepted members of the community. In contrast, Mokshith and Dhruv wore sky-blue outfits, a gift from another spiritual institution. During this period, diverse spiritual practices thrived, and since they were unattached to any specific school, they could explore and experience as many as they wanted. Both boys, orphans living in the forest without proper shelter, perceived no differences among the birds and animals surrounding them.

They presented fresh lotus flowers to one of the disciples, requesting that he offer them to the Enlightened One, the singularly recognised enlightened figure of their era, who was acclaimed as the Master of all. The boys found a place in the crowd where anyone could participate in the gathering — to listen to speeches, pose spiritual inquiries, and enjoy the meals provided by the disciples after the event concluded. However, to gain membership in the community, they had to demonstrate a certain level of spirituality and intellectual capability, a demanding and rigorous process.

Dhruv watched the enlightened one from afar, seated upon the stone chair.

"Hey, Mokshith, check out the Master; he shines so brightly. He truly is a master for all of us. One day, I will undoubtedly be his favourite student."

However, Mokshith was not interested in Dhruv's excitement and did not pay attention. Instead, he inquired when the food would be served and expressed his frustration that it would have been nice if they had offered food before the congregation began.

"Did you hear what I said? You're not worth having serious discussions with," Dhruv said, clearly frustrated.

"Look, Dhruv, what seems serious to you might not be to others. I understand your admiration for that Master; that's your choice. However, I don't share the same feelings. I'm not interested in pursuing a spiritual path. My focus here is just on two things: food and you. That's it."

"Students, it's time for the Master to address you. Please maintain silence and pay attention. After his speech, you can ask questions, but remember to be courteous," instructed the disciple in charge of upholding peace among the group.

When the enlightened one opened his eyes, everyone in that hall paid very intense focus to what he was going to deliver. His voice resonated with wisdom and compassion, and his speech emanated enlightenment.

"Wisdom can be acquired in two distinct ways: the straightforward way and the challenging way. The straightforward way consists of observing the actions of others and learning from their errors while imagining yourself in similar situations. In contrast, the challenging way is more complex and personal, requiring direct involvement through your own experiences. This is the challenging path. So, which will you choose?" the enlightened one asked the audience.

A student from the open hall stood and declared, "Master, I choose the first method."

Laughter erupted from everyone, Dhruv and Mokshith included.

"What method will you select?" Dhruv inquired.

"I won't choose either option. I'll follow my heart, then I'll let go and move forward," Mokshith replied confidently.

They both laughed, but soon, silence enveloped the crowd. Dhruv and Mokshith understood why, and the others did too. A figure stood on a rock at least ten feet tall in the back, where the enlightened one was seated. He was barely visible, completely unclothed with muddy hair and skin, resembling a natural entity.

"Is God present?" he inquired the enlightened one."

Everyone in the hall was eager to hear the enlightened one's reply, but the enlightened one stayed silent. Eventually, the naked person burst into laughter and exited the area.

"The gathering has ended. Please savour your first meal before you leave," the Disciple announced while organising the assembly.

After the food was served, everyone helped themselves and found seats. As Dhruv and Mokshith received their meals on banana leaves, Dhruv asked a disciple if the enlightened one had accepted them into the community. The disciple informed him that acceptance would take time and urged them to give the enlightened one space to decide. Frustrated, Mokshith pressed for a timeline. Dhruv, in a stern tone, told him to be quiet and led him away. Each time Mokshith acted out, Dhruv made it a point to rein him in.

At night, Dhruv and Mokshith reclined on the rock. Mokshith looked up at the sky, resting his arms behind his head as he marvelled at the stars. The water flowed softly, producing a soothing sound. In the distance, wolves howled, with insects and owls adding their calls.

"Why does he come daily? He just stands there. Upon his arrival, silence descends among us, and he poses a single question: "Is God there?" The Master stays quiet, neither affirming nor denying. I just can't grasp it. If I were to ask you, you wouldn't share anything about him," Mokshith remarked.

"Are you going to let me sleep or not?" Dhruv inquired.

Mokshith promptly shut his eyes to pretend to be asleep.

"He's quite materialistic and won't believe anything unless he sees it himself," Dhruv said, his voice sleepy as he kept his eyes shut.

Mokshith then rose, shifted to his side, propped his right hand on the ground, and rested his palm against his right ear.

"How is that possible? We can't see everything. So many things remain impossible for us to perceive with our eyes," Mokshith said.

Dhruv responded, "That's right; he only recognises what falls within his own experience."

"That may be true, but how can we conclude if something is beyond our ability to experience?" said Mokshith.

"If you discuss that matter with him, he will convince you and change your nature."

"Can anyone be changed by his influence?"

"Not everyone, just you," Dhruv said.

"Why just me?"

"Because you're foolish. Now, quiet your thoughts and go to sleep," said Dhruv.

Mokshith, feeling disappointed, shut his eyes and drifted off to sleep. In the complete darkness, the sole sound was the gentle flow of water nearby. Slowly, even that sound started to diminish.

Total darkness...

Chapter 4

The Strange Sound

Anvesh lay on the ground, leaves gently falling one by one onto his face, trying to wake him. Yet those cascading leaves were not enough to rouse him. His eyes began to roll without warning as a strange sound gradually reached him from afar. The sound intensified until it filled the air with such volume that he quickly sat up and covered his ears to block it out. It was a loud, streaming sound; however, it did not resemble water. He felt something new, something he had never experienced before. He remained there for a while, his hands pressed to his ears. Although he covered them completely, he could still hear that strange sound from outside. After some time, the sound faded away, and he let his hands drop from his ears before slowly opening his eyes. Anvesh looked around and realised he was sitting in the forest, with giant trees blocking the sunlight completely. He could perceive the sound of a gentle stream coming from beneath the ground where he sat. He quickly got up and moved further away from that spot. Leaning down, he pressed his ears to the ground and listened intently. He heard the heavy flow of a stream beneath him, prompting him to rise immediately as if he might sink into it. Anvesh moved into an area surrounded by trees as tall as he was, finding himself encircled by clusters of those trees. Unfortunately, he could hear the distant sound of the stream, louder than in his previous location. Suddenly, that sound vanished. Doubting the trees that surrounded him, he approached one of the nearby ones, pressing his ear against the trunk to listen. He detected a strong, loud sound of the stream emanating from within the trunk. Alarmed, he quickly retreated, stumbling into another tree and falling to the ground. Noticing a small trickle of water, he began to follow that stream. Eventually, it led him to a pond. When he saw the pond, he felt thirsty, took a handful of water, and started to drink. As he swallowed, he felt strange. His throat began to burn, and he screamed loudly. But that burning sensation transformed into a sweet taste, leaving him utterly confused. Looking at his hands, he noticed they weren't wet from the water. Disturbed, he wanted to test it further, so he waded into the pond up to his knees. When he pulled his legs out, they were scorched. Shocked, he quickly got up and tried to leave that area. Yet, no matter which direction he walked in, he found himself returning to the same pond repeatedly. Realising he was trapped in the middle of the forest, he sat down in front of the pond and stared at the water, lost in thought. The sound of the stream roared in his ears once more. Closing his eyes and covering his ears, he sat there calmly.

Total darkness…

Chapter 5

From Home To Village

"**M**aster! What is desire? How can we liberate ourselves from wanting? Can someone truly exist without desire?" inquired a student from the congregation hall.

All eyes were on the master, waiting for his response to that question.

"It is impossible for a seeker to be without desire. If there is seeking within you, then desire will occupy your mind. Desire should arise from within you, not from others. Self-derived desire is genuine and a more powerful energy that keeps you alert."

While the master spoke on desire, Mokshith's eyes wandered to the golden boxes next to him.

"Our master remained untouched by material possessions; however, why was gold all around him, held in such high regard and celebrated by those near him? Do these illusions not envelop him?" Mokshith pondered, captivated by the golden boxes.

"Master never requested anyone to keep gold close to him. To him, gold is valued the same as stone. Yet, those boxes represent the worth determined by the people who revere him," Dhruv responded.

However, Mokshith kept gazing at the golden boxes instead of focusing on the teachings of the enlightened one.

Suddenly, the light from the boxes grew dim, and the glow surrounding the enlightened one diminished, too. A naked man appeared behind the master. The usual radiance that surrounded the enlightened one disappeared, and he stopped shining. The entire congregation fell silent, eager to hear the naked man's question. Everyone was intrigued by the nature of the inquiry he would direct at the master this time. Mokshith speculated that the naked man's question for the enlightened one would be, "Is God present?"

"Who are you?" the naked man inquired.

Once again, the master stayed silent. The congregation fell quiet for a moment, and the naked man laughed heartily before leaving. Later, as Mokshith and Dhruv got ready to depart, one of the disciples approached them and said, "Tomorrow, before sunset, you both must head east and stay in the village."

"For what purpose? How can we locate the village you mentioned?" Mokshith asked the disciple.

"Choose your words carefully, Mokshith," Dhruv warned. "I apologise for his lack of understanding."

"As you embark on your journey east, you will reach the village I mentioned by sunset. There, a merchant requires your help. You must remain until he discovers what he seeks. If you succeed in your return, the master will give you news," the Disciple explained.

"Will it be good news?" Mokshith asked again, his curiosity evident in his voice.

"That depends on how you interpret the information—good or bad," replied Disciple.

Dhruv strongly desired to prove himself and join the master's program, while Mokshith looked forward to discovering new experiences.

"Could I ask one more question? If we successfully complete the task you assigned us, will we become permanent members of this school? Is this a test for us?" Mokshith queried.

"Set out on your journeys. They can change your life. Who knows?" said Disciple as he departed.

Dhruv and Mokshith shared inquisitive looks, wondering what the future might hold for them.

Beneath the full moon at night, Mokshith reclined on a rock, contemplating the celestial glow. Dhruv, having just completed his meditation, was getting ready for sleep.

"At last, the moment has arrived for us to demonstrate our capabilities, Dhruv. If we accomplish this task successfully, we can stop worrying about food and shelter," exclaimed Mokshith with enthusiasm.

Dhruv, aware of his wild uncertainties, refrained from joining Mokshith's discussion. Thus, he stayed quiet and got ready for sleep.

"I still find it hard to understand. That man in the village is rich and has everything he could want in life. What more can we give him? We are just monks."

"Nobody in this world possesses everything. To gain one thing, you have to sacrifice another. You must let go to receive," Dhruv said.

"If we are content with what we possess, why should we fret over what we've lost? We need to be mindful when selecting the right things to cherish and determining what it is appropriate to release," stated Mokshith.

"Sometimes, compromises are necessary in life," said Dhruv.

"Could you give me an example?" Mokshith inquired, his curiosity growing.

"Currently, I'm with you. If I truly wanted peace, I would leave without hesitation and distance myself from you permanently. Yet, I choose not to do so. This illustrates a clear example of someone who is compromised in life."

As Mokshith continued to reflect, he posed more questions to Dhruv.

Dhruv interjected, urging, "Calm your mind. We must reach the village before sunset tomorrow. It's time to rest. Let's sleep now."

They woke up early, around 2 a.m., which is the usual time for monks to rise. They packed their food because they were informed that their journey would challenge their endurance. Mokshith glanced at Dhruv, who was absorbed in his packing. Doubts swirled in Mokshith's mind, and he wanted to seek clarity from Dhruv, but he hesitated, fearing he might make him angry. Thus, he kept silent.

They started their journey without worrying about the destination. As they left the hill that used to be their home, Mokshith paused, turned back, and took one last look at it.

"Mokshith, what happened?"

"I never thought I would ever leave our home," Mokshith expressed, feeling a deep sense of loss for his place.

"Worry not; this could be our last departure from home. I hope we never have to leave it again in the future. Let's go now," Dhruv urged.

They started their journey again.

"Our master often reminds us, 'Some journeys result in happiness, while others may lead to sadness. Reflect on this: what will we attain from this journey—joy or sorrow?'"

Dhruv replied, "If I travel alone, I will return unchanged. But now that I am going with you, I will come back burdened with immense sorrow."

"Anyhow, whatever you are going to experience is going to be because of me. So you should show gratitude to me," Mokshith declared assertively.

While heading to their destination, Mokshith's incessant chatter started to irritate Dhruv. At last, they reached the village entrance and gazed around in wonder at the strange arrangement of houses, a sight unlike anything they had encountered before since they had never wandered far from the hills they called home.

Mokshith faced Dhruv with resolve, stating, "The sun is nearly down, and there's no one here to welcome us. What should we do now?"

"Mokshith, avoid jumping to conclusions too fast. Look over there. Someone is coming. He could lead us to the wealthy man's house."

As the figure drew near, they noticed he held a lamp in one hand and a pair of blankets in the other.

"Are you coming from the enlightened one?"

"Yes," Mokshith replied immediately, as though the person before them was about to take them to the merchant's house.

"My name is Raghu; I am the servant of the landlord, Dhanvanth. Please let me guide you to his residence."

They began to follow Raghu. Mokshith noticed that as they started moving, darkness quickly obscured the sun, and the entire village was enveloped in fog, making it impossible for them to see Raghu. However, Raghu swiftly lit the lamp in his hand.

"Are you feeling cold? I brought blankets because the temperature in this village can drop significantly after sunset."

Mokshith replied, "No, thank you. We are used to much colder conditions than this."

Raghu remained silent and kept walking, while Mokshith and Dhruv expected him to talk. He stayed quiet until they reached the wealthy man's residence, stopping in front of the largest house in the village. Raghu pointed to a home next to the extravagant mansion and said, "Our owner has arranged for you to stay here. Everything is prepared for you inside. Have a restful night. Please let me know the best time for our owner to visit you."

Dhruv replied, "He can come after sunrise."

The man left in silence. Dhruv and Mokshith stepped into the house. The unique ambience struck them, as they had never been in such a cosy and radiant setting. Having lived in the outdoors, they were accustomed to sleeping on bare rocks. Mokshith rushed to a lamp filled with shimmering liquid, captivated by the dancing flames.

"Dhruv, look! I've seen this type of light in the master's hall," he exclaimed, hurrying to the lamp resting on a stone chair. Filled with excitement, Mokshith pressed his hand against the wall, experimenting with the shadow cast by the lamp. His hand appeared gigantic as he wiggled his fingers, becoming entranced by the shadows.

"Mokshith, please concentrate. We have a lot of work tomorrow. Could you stop being childish and turn off that lamp? I need to sleep."

Mokshith stopped his playful antics and lay down on the floor next to Dhruv in that room. Together, they slowly vanished into the darkness.

Total Darkness…

Chapter 6

Step Into The Dark

The sound of a stream gradually approached him from a distance. It reached his ears, prompting Anvesh to open his eyes. He sat upright and checked himself—he was at the top of the mountain, and that astonished him. Then, he began to observe his surroundings. From this height, everything appeared small to him. He couldn't recall how long it took him to climb this mountain. He remembered shutting his eyes and reopening them; everything happened in that time of darkness. He struggled to understand what occurred each time he awoke in the forest. As far as he could see, nothing but the dense trees were visible. He realised he had lost his way. Perhaps he had chosen the first route, but his journey had led him down a second path that needed to be forged. Sitting in complete stillness and allowing his mind to wander, he heard the sound of a heavy stream behind him. He looked back to find its source but couldn't. Turning completely around, he stood up and began walking toward the sound, disregarding the path he had followed; he simply moved toward the sound of the stream. The surroundings grew darker, pulling him deeper into the gloom. He paused to think again, with the sound guiding him along the shadowy path. He worried about the unknown destination he might reach by traversing through the darkness. He didn't want to go there; he aimed to reach the enlightened one's institute. All of a sudden, he noticed footprints on the dark path. The footprints glowed. He could only see the illuminated traces left behind in the all-encompassing darkness. He was torn between returning and searching the entire forest, which could take at least fifteen years, or stepping further into the darkness toward an uncertain destination. He didn't want to waste another fifteen years in that forest. He closed his eyes, took a deep breath, opened them, and put his right foot into the glowing footprint. When he placed his foot upon it, he was shocked to discover that the footprint matched his own. That footprint belonged to him. He was astonished because he had never been there before. He immediately took his foot off that footprint and looked around for anyone, but all he could see was complete darkness. Although he felt scared, he chose to walk further. He could see nothing but the footprints as he ventured deeper into the darkness. Slowly, he started to discern something resembling tree branches swaying gently on both sides of his path as the soft wind brushed against them. However, those moving shapes were swallowed by shadows. He continued a bit further and realised they were indeed real trees with branches. As he suspected, the tree branches danced in the wind. He pressed on. After a while, he halted when he noticed old, tattered white clothes hanging from the branches. There were so many ragged pieces on numerous branches that it seemed as though someone had wandered through the trees, causing the branches to tear their clothes apart in a failed attempt to dress themselves. He was completely bewildered, unsure of what was happening. He pressed on, careful not to touch those garments.

Complete darkness enveloped him. He could only hear the sound of the stream. He blindly followed the footprints, placing his foot on each one. He kept going... going... going. Gradually, the sound of the stream faded away. There was total silence and darkness. He could no longer take a single step forward because he could neither see his footprints nor hear the sound of the stream. He realised that the footprints had not guided him down this path; it was the stream. He stood in the dark, waiting for the stream to lead him further. The darkness completely surrounded him.

Total Darkness…

Chapter 7

Sreevalli

In the early morning, Dhruv sat facing east, deeply engaged in meditation. About six feet in front of him, Mokshith slept soundly. After a while, Dhruv opened his eyes and observed him. He glanced out the window beside him, taking in Mokshith's position. Dhruv then got up and opened the window to let the sunlight in, which gently illuminated Mokshith's face. Despite his love for the sun, Mokshith remained undisturbed. Although he had been sleeping on the jungle floor, he now lay on a remarkably comfortable bed, making it hard for his body to wake up. Dhruv intended to scold him awake; however, a sudden knock at the door interrupted his thoughts. At the sound, Mokshith sat up quickly as if he had an internal alarm for that noise. He instantly assumed a meditative pose but was still half-asleep in his seated position.

"May I come in?" the servant asked softly.

"Yes, please come in," replied Dhruv.

The servant stepped inside, disregarding their circumstances as he began delivering his message.

"My master, Dhanvanth, is ready to meet you now. Is this a convenient time for him to enter?" he inquired.

"Yes, certainly. Please let him in. We are expecting him," Dhruv responded.

After the servant left and closed the door, Mokshith stood up quickly, looking at Dhruv with worry as if expecting a severe scolding. However, Dhruv didn't scold him. Instead, he turned his attention to Dhanvanth, waiting for his arrival. Dhruv experienced a wave of nervousness, acutely aware of his lack of experience as a preacher and that he was merely an acquaintance of the enlightened one. He put his anxiety aside. As he entered the room, Dhanvanth surveyed the space and gazed at Dhruv, who was sitting thoughtfully on a stone chair.

"Please, come in," Dhruv said, closing his eyes and sitting in a meditative posture.

Dhanvanth nodded, looking both formal and relieved.

"I hope you both had a pleasant night."

"Indeed, we appreciate your hospitality," Dhruv replied, preserving the tranquil atmosphere around him.

Dhanvanth's face showed a hint of gratitude.

"I kindly request that you convey my gratitude to the enlightened one for bringing you here to assist me."

Dhruv opened his eyes, smiled gently at Dhanvanth, and said, "Helping our master's followers is our duty."

Dhanvanth smiled back at Dhruv with thankfulness.

"Please share with me what is bothering you," Dhruv asked.

Dhanvanth felt a bit reluctant to discuss his issue with Mokshith present and wished for him to leave. Noticing Dhanvanth's discomfort, Dhruv shared a silent understanding with Mokshith, who left the room to provide some privacy. Once the door closed, the landlord

hurried to Dhruv and knelt down, tears flowing
from his eyes.

"I have wealth, family, and influential
friends. I can dominate anyone if I wish. Yet, I
struggle to find peace; my eyes cannot rest.
Despite possessing everything, insecurity
plagues me. Even in the presence of those who
care for me, fear persists. Master, please relieve
my suffering and eliminate its source,"
Dhanvanth pleaded.

"You have put in relentless effort to
build your wealth, influence, and the affection of
those around you. To release yourself from these
attachments, significant suffering is required.
Achieving peace is not an overnight process.
Now, go and rest for a while. Remember,
patience is essential for this journey," Dhruv
advised.

Mokshith hid behind the door, listening
to everything happening in the conversation
inside the room. All of a sudden, Mokshith heard
the sound of the door opening. Then, he
immediately tried to escape from that place. As a
result, he entered a garden filled with beautiful

flowers. Mokshith was captivated by the beauty of that garden. He touched one flower in that garden and felt how soft it was. He had never experienced such delicacy in a flower before. Since he came from the wild, there were not only animals; even flowers were untouched. They had to protect themselves as they were not cared for by humans. Nature had made them adapt to survive on their own. He spotted a peacock spreading its tail feathers and beginning to dance. Mokshith began to appreciate the beauty of the peacock. Suddenly, he noticed a young woman hiding behind the dancing bird and peeking out, trying to follow the peacock's movements while hoping not to be discovered by anyone nearby. Mokshith observed two peacocks dancing in sync. As she peeked out, she noticed Mokshith standing and signalled for him to keep her presence a secret. Just as he tried to understand her signal, a girl about ten years old unexpectedly stepped in front of him. She diligently searched until she spotted Mokshith standing there.

"Where is she?" she asked sharply.

Mokshith was startled by her intense tone and pointed toward the peacock that was dancing.

When she noticed the dancing peacock, she clapped loudly to frighten it off. As expected, it took to the skies, revealing a figure that had been concealed behind it.

Mokshith's breath momentarily caught as he looked at her. She was breathtaking, and he found it hard to look away. Since he had never encountered a young woman before, he was uncertain about how to respond to her allure. While he appreciated the beauty of nature, the enchantment of a young woman was a new experience for him, filling him with a mix of unfamiliar emotions.

"Hey, sister! I found you!" the younger girl shouted happily while sprinting toward her beautiful sister. Grabbing her hand, she exclaimed, "I found you! As promised, it's time for you to take me out to play with my friends. Let's hurry and not waste any more time."

Sreevalli, the charming elder sister, smiled and said, "Alright, let's head out now."

The siblings shared their names: Sreevalli, the 20-year-old elder sister, and Lakshmi, the 10-year-old younger sister.

While passing Mokshith, Sreevalli abruptly stopped and inquired, "Who are you?"

Mokshith was surprised and momentarily speechless, as he didn't anticipate being spoken to directly.

"I'm speaking to you, man. Who are you, and why are you here?" she asked.

In the end, Mokshith composed himself and said, "I am Mokshith. My friend and I are here for your father."

"My mother mentioned that two monks would come to our house. Where's your friend?"

"He's in that room, speaking with your father."

"Alright, we're heading out. Come along!"

"You two, where are you headed?"

Sreevalli didn't respond to him. Instead, she grabbed his hand and started walking away, pulling him along. As she did, Mokshith felt an unfamiliar sensation in his body, one he had never encountered, even in his dreams. He remained stunned for a moment. They exited the house and made their way to the place where Lakshmi chose to play with her friends. Walking side by side, Mokshith quietly listened to their discussion.

While chatting, Sreevalli glanced at Mokshith and asked, "I indicated you shouldn't disclose my hiding place to her, yet you ignored it. Why did you tell her?"

"I always tell the truth," Mokshith replied.

"What!" Sreevalli exclaimed, surprised by his response.

"Sister, we lie so often every day that we can't even count them," said Lakshmi. They both laughed, but Mokshith didn't understand why the lying was funny.

"Do you always wear this dress, or do you only wear it occasionally?" Sreevalli asked.

"This is what we wear. What I'm wearing now is something anyone can wear. However, once someone becomes a member of the School of the Enlightened One, they must wear white permanently."

"It doesn't matter if you're from that school or not. You all should wear the same outfit for your entire life, right?"

"Yes," Mokshith admitted.

"If I were in your position, I would definitely run away from that place without even informing anyone," Sreevalli said firmly.

Mokshith laughed at what she said. They continued talking, walking, and laughing together until they reached their destination, where the giant trees stood in nature's orderly arrangement. The branches of each tree buzzed with swings and girls playing together. When Lakshmi saw them having fun, she couldn't contain her excitement. She quickly grabbed Sreevalli's hand and pulled her toward the joy.

"Lakshmi, I need to tell you something. I informed our mother that we were heading to music class and would return in the evening. If you happen to hurt yourself here, it could be the last day you play with them. Remember, our mother will never allow you to play outside again," Sreevalli warned her younger sister.

"Sister, don't waste your energy warning me. I won't care about what you say right now. Let's go play together!"

Mokshith understood that he should wait for them till they finished playing. Mokshith found a small lotus pond entirely surrounded by flowering trees. He sat on a flat stone in front of the pond. He began to observe the flowers and leaves from the trees falling rhythmically onto the pond, creating ripples on the surface. He was amazed by how nature was perfectly organised. It was as if the gentle wind had asked those flowers and leaves to be like paintbrushes, crafting a beautiful painting. However, Mokshith wasn't lost in thought. He shifted his focus and gazed at Sreevalli, who was playing with Lakshmi and her friends. Sreevalli noticed Mokshith watching her. At first, she ignored him, but then she realised he was focused solely on her. She left the group and hurried over to him, placing her hands on her hips in mock anger.

"Hey, why are you staring at me? Haven't you ever seen a young woman before?"

"I have heard of girls like you but haven't seen any. You are the first girl I have ever seen and touched," said Mokshith, gazing strangely into her eyes.

She laughed at him for referring to her as a girl.

"I couldn't help but look at you. I don't know what it is," Mokshith admitted. Sreevalli is intrigued by his innocence.

"I know what it is!" she said playfully. "So, why do I always want to look at you? I've tried so many times not to, but my efforts have been useless."

Sreevalli laughed when he said that.

"Okay, now tell me why you both came to my house and what you need from my father."

"We came to help your father," Mokshith explained.

"'To help my father?!' She laughed in disbelief, her voice ringing with incredulity. My father is the most powerful landlord in this village. When he desires something, nothing can impede him. He possesses everything. What more could you possibly offer him?"

"No one has everything in life; only they can know what is missing within themselves," Mokshith responded thoughtfully.

Sreevalli contemplated this. "Alright, then tell me—what am I thinking about right now?" she challenged.

Mokshith tried to explain at first but was unsure of how to answer.

"I'm sorry, I cannot tell you what you think."

"Exactly! We can't even know what we want, so how can we help others ease their pain?" Sreevalli remarked.

Mokshith fell into deep thought.

Just then, Lakshmi shouted, "I'm feeling hungry! Let's go home now!"

"Okay, come on, let's go," Sreevalli said as she left the pond area, but Mokshith remained lost in thought. His eyes were fixed on the surface of the pond, yet he wasn't truly seeing it. He would have noticed the flowers falling onto the water if he had been focused. Instead, he was absorbed in Sreevalli's words. He contemplated how our senses are merely the servants of the mind. For many generations, spiritual seekers have tried to understand that our senses are enslaved by our minds or that our minds are enslaved by our senses.

The Enlightened One

"Waves from the ocean continuously flow back and forth to surpass the shore. They are never calm. Similarly, human minds behave like the ocean's waves; no wave remains still, and no human mind is ever at rest or in tranquillity."

The landlord sat across from Dhruv, who remained in a meditative position while preaching.

Dhruv

Humans are constantly drawn to love, pain, sadness, happiness, family, betrayal, anger, guilt, and countless other emotions. People believe their experiences are real, yet these are all illusions. They create these feelings and convince themselves that they are genuine. One must have a teacher to manage them. Some seek a teacher outside, while others find a teacher within themselves. To discover peace within, you must face and navigate the waves of the ocean. Once you pass through the waves and reach the ocean's centre, you will find a waveless ocean within you. For a tranquil mind, peace comes naturally and without effort. To such a mind, there is no distinction between happiness and sadness; both hold no weight.

Meanwhile, Mokshith grew closer to Sreevalli. His daily routine involved waking up early to accompany her while Dhruv prepared to share his teachings. Throughout the day, Mokshith spent time with Sreevalli and returned home later in the evening. The only times Dhruv acknowledged Mokshith were when he left their room in the morning and when he returned to sleep at night. Mokshith slipped into the room quietly, like a cat sneaking in to steal food. He checked to see if Dhruv was asleep, then silently lay beside him, smiling as he recalled the day spent with Sreevalli and felt excited about seeing her again the next day.

Thirty days had passed since Dhruv and Mokshith arrived in the village. During this time, much has transpired. The landlord has made progress in his studies to alleviate his pain, and Dhruv has gained confidence in becoming a preacher. He firmly believed he would be a permanent member of The Enlightened One's School and was excited about the prospect of sharing preaching efforts with Mokshith, as he wished to remain close to him.

After a week, having just finished his lesson, Dhruv expressed his happiness: "I am thrilled that you have improved so much. I believe my teachings have been beneficial in easing your pain and initiating your spiritual journey."

"I feel so calm now, Master. Thank you for being so considerate," the landlord replied.

Dhruv did not probe further but offered him a warm smile instead.

As the landlord prepared to leave the room, he paused and turned back. "Master, I'm sorry—I forgot to mention something."

Dhruv regarded him with curiosity but kept his thoughts to himself.

"Our master, the enlightened one, has sent word that he wishes for you to be there by tomorrow evening," the landlord said.

Once the landlord exited the room, Dhruv's excitement bubbled over, and he was filled with questions about whether he would become a permanent member of the school or a leading disciple. His mind wandered aimlessly for a moment, and he felt a strong urge to find Mokshith. Good or bad news aside, Mokshith was the only person he wanted to share it with. He searched the entire village for him, eager to see how Mokshith would react to the news of their impending return.

Dhruv eventually found Mokshith sitting quietly in front of a pond beneath the trees, watching the flowers fall. However, he was not alone; he held Sreevalli's hand while she leaned her head on his shoulder. They sat in silence, communicating in

a way that only they understood. Dhruv found a
spot behind a nearby tree to observe them,
unaware of what he would discover.

"I will talk to my mother tomorrow,"
Sreevalli said.

"What about your father?" Mokshith
asked.

"Once my mother says okay, my father
will accept us," Sreevalli replied.

Mokshith, filled with emotion but trying
not to reveal it, said, "I'm scared. Will they
accept me as your future husband, knowing I
have nothing? I am a monk and don't want to be
a monk anymore."

"Don't worry; everything will be fine.
We will be so happy together. I don't want to
lose you. I want to marry you and have children
with you," Sreevalli said, her voice filled with
deep emotion.

Mokshith looked at her, tears welling in
his eyes.

Dhruv was shocked because he didn't
expect that they were in love. He quietly left the
scene without hesitation. Sunset marked the time

for Mokshith to enter the room. As usual, he stepped inside and found Dhruv in a sleeping position. Mokshith quietly settled beside him, ensuring that Dhruv remained asleep. Although Dhruv had his eyes closed, he was far from sleeping. As Mokshith closed his eyes, memories of the day flooded back, and he tried to envision a happier tomorrow.

"Tomorrow, we're heading back to our place," Dhruv said.

Mokshith was taken aback. He sat up, turned to look at him, and asked, "Dhruv, did the landlord find peace?"

"We must be in front of the master by tomorrow evening; he sent us a message. Now, sleep," Dhruv insisted.

Mokshith lay back down, closing his eyes, but today's memories and tomorrow's hopes morphed into unexpected sorrow. He dreaded the sunrise, wishing the night would linger forever.

However, the sun rose early for Mokshith. Both of them packed their belongings in that room. Dhruv observed Mokshith, who appeared unprepared to go back. Suddenly, they heard an argument approaching from a distance.

"Let me go inside and kick that idiot out! How dare he do this!" shouted Parvathi, Sreevalli's mother.

"Mother, please control yourself. He didn't do anything. It's not his mistake. I loved him," said Sreevalli.

"Just keep quiet. It's not your fault; it's his fault," she said, pointing at her husband, the wealthy Dhanvanth.

"He never denied you anything. Truly, this is his fault," Sreevalli's mother added, anger evident in her voice.

"Please don't shout like that. They will hear," Dhanvanth said, requesting that she refrain from yelling at them.

They all stood in front of the door while Dhruv and Mokshith remained inside the room. Both of them felt scared.

"Please calm down. We shouldn't make any decisions when we are angry. Stay calm, and we will discuss them," said Dhanvanth.

"What are you talking about? Do we need to speak with them? What should we say? Are you really going to let our daughter marry that monk? Are you out of your mind? If we proceed with this, do you realize how much our reputation in this village will suffer? Have you considered how these people will view us? These monks are like beggars; they have nothing in their lives," Parvathi exclaimed angrily.

"Do we truly have everything in our lives? Do you believe we are happy now? No, we are merely living for others. We think about others daily, how they will react, and how we conform to their expectations," said Dhanvanth.

"He is a nice guy, and I would be happy if I married him," said Sreevalli.

Mokshith's eyes brimmed with tears at Sreevalli's words.

"OK, now I realise you've all made your decision. So, there's no need to argue anymore. You can do whatever you want; you can go inside and talk to him and let our daughter marry him. But before that, you'll have to cross my dead body to do that."

Parvathi suddenly revealed a knife hidden behind her, which frightened them. She then ran far away to prevent them from taking it.

"Mother, please put that knife down now!" Sreevalli shouted, tears streaming down her cheeks.

Mokshith and Dhruv felt terrified inside and exchanged fearful glances.

"Don't come any closer to me. If you do, I'll end my life. Why are you worrying about me? You don't need to consider me at all. You can do whatever you wish. Just go now," Parvathi said firmly.

"Mother, please, if you harm yourself, I will surely die. Now put down that knife," Sreevalli said.

"Alright then. Promise me you'll forget him and never meet him again. Promise me now," Parvathi said authoritatively.

Sreevalli fell silent for a moment. Dhruv looked at Mokshith thoughtfully and curiously, awaiting Sreevalli's response.

After closing her eyes and taking a deep breath, she said, "OK, Mother, as you wish. From now on, he will no longer be in my heart. I will forget him and will never meet him again. Please put down that knife now."

That's it; Mokshith realised that everything he had imagined had collapsed. Dhruv looked at Mokshith with concern, but Mokshith didn't meet his gaze because he lacked the strength to lift his head and face Dhruv. Gradually, the conversations outside began to fade away. They all left the place, and silence lingered for a moment. In a flash, a knock sounded at the door of Dhruv and Mokshith's room. Both felt tension as they didn't know who it was.

"Who is that?" Dhruv asked.

"I am a servant. Can I come inside now?"

"Yes, please come in," said Dhruv.

He came inside and said, "You both need to leave now. Our owner, Parvathi, has ordered me to take you out now. Shall we?"

"Yes, we are ready," said Dhruv.

Both Dhruv and Mokshith emerged from the house. Mokshith paused, turned back, gazed at the house, closed his eyes, and recalled all the memories of Sreevalli within it.

"Mokshith, let's leave this place," said Dhruv.

Chapter 8

Different Wounds, Same Pain

They both left the village, walking side by side toward their destination. Although the sunlight was harsh, the banyan trees lining their path provided shelter. Dhruv glanced at Mokshith, eager to discuss something. However, Mokshith appeared disinterested in the conversation, his steps heavy as if reluctant to go home. While his feet moved forward, his mind seemed to pull him back. Finally, Dhruv stepped in front of Mokshith, blocking his way to prevent him from walking further. Dhruv looked at Mokshith, but Mokshith kept his gaze directed downward. Dhruv put his hand on Mokshith's shoulder and started to talk.

"My friend, please don't remain silent like that. Allow your pain to be expressed from within you. The more you keep your feelings bottled up, the more you will hurt yourself. Observe the people living in that village. Everyone there is suffering from severe mental illness. They have formed a circle of illusions and reside within it, believing that the circle is real. Do you want to be one of them? Please come out of your illusions, my friend."

"Are we truly living in the real world, Dhruv? Or are we merely prisoners of an elaborate illusion?" Look at those people in that village—they embrace every moment, daring to experience life to the fullest. They have the chance to learn and grow from their choices. But what do we have? Just hollow words echoing in the void. I'm not expressing all of this because she isn't in my life. "The moments I shared with her are enough to allow me to live the rest of my life happily," said Mokshith, closing his eyes and trying to hide the pain that was ready to burst within.

"Happily? Are you foolish? That is not happiness. That happiness is like a fleeting breeze; it comes and goes in an instant. After that, you will find yourself in misery forever. Don't let yourself be trapped in temporary happiness."

"Then tell me, what is permanent happiness?

Do you believe that escaping reality constitutes true happiness? No, that is not happiness, my friend. That is cowardice. Such a life is merely an illusion. In their lives, they have experiences. They take actions, learn from those actions, and acquire real knowledge. But what are we doing, running away from them, living separately, doing nothing, and calling ourselves better people than they are?"

Dhruv stared at Mokshith in disbelief, never expecting to hear those words from him.

"You can't understand it, Dhruv, because you have never loved anyone in your life. So, how could you comprehend the pain of losing a loved one?"

"Master was right. This journey caused you pain. I can see how much you were affected by these people for a few days in that village. You are a coward and a weak-minded person."

"It's amusing that you're calling me a coward. But what about you, Dhruv? You go to that school every day, begging for food and shelter. Your life's goal is to become part of that school because you're afraid of being alone. You dread ending up lonely. Even now, you're not worried about me; instead, you're fixated on what might happen if I return, marry her, and live happily with her without coming back to you. You're afraid of losing me, Dhruv. You don't want anyone to be happy; you want everyone to suffer as you do from insecurity. You are incredibly selfish."

Dhruv didn't reply and remained silent.

Regret washed over Mokshith almost immediately as he noticed the change in Dhruv's expression. His friend's head dropped, tears welling in his eyes. A pang of guilt pierced Mokshith's heart. Then, without warning, Dhruv slapped him across the face—a shock that sent ripples through the tense atmosphere. But Mokshith didn't react to Dhruv. The slap didn't inflict the pain that Mokshith felt. He moved away and sat under the banyan tree in a meditative posture, beginning to meditate in order to escape the memories of Sreevalli that kept flooding his mind. Meditation is a traditional practice among monks for observing their thoughts and understanding their origins. Monks who truly excel in meditation can dispel unwanted thoughts from their minds. Yet, in his case, meditation was failing to free him from Sreevalli's memories.

Dhruv sat under a tree facing Mokshith, who was battling to push away thoughts of Sreevalli. Memories poured from Mokshith's closed eyelids like tears. Dhruv couldn't help but smirk at Mokshith, though he felt a twinge of sympathy. As Dhruv looked at Mokshith, he slowly dwelled on his past, where a lonely five-year-old boy often cried, desiring companionship but being reluctant to reach out. This isolated child sat in fear of his environment until a kind-hearted ten-year-old approached, offering comfort, sharing his snack, and inviting him to play. The older boy took the five-year-old on his lap during terrifying nightmares, becoming a father figure to him. At that moment, the ten-year-old boy watched the five-year-old meditating and struggling to focus.

Tears filled Dhruv's eyes as he observed. Eventually, Mokshith realised he wouldn't find peace through meditation. Frustrated, he got up and began his journey back. They didn't walk side by side as they had on their way to the village; instead, Mokshith walked ahead while Dhruv lingered about ten feet behind.

Arriving in the evening, they met the enlightened one in his chamber. When they stood before him, he did not speak and instructed his disciples to let them leave. They returned too late to sleep that night, as they usually go to bed at sunset.

They lay on the rock where they used to sleep. Mokshith closed his eyes, unsure if he was truly asleep. The gentle sound of flowing water separated them. Dhruv, unable to sleep, watched Mokshith. The animals were quiet that night; while they may not have perceived the sounds, they could hear the water flowing between them.

Early in the morning, the birds attempted to awaken Dhruv. He slowly opened his eyes, searching for Mokshith, almost as if he had conditioned himself to do so. But Mokshith was nowhere to be found. Dhruv jumped up in shock and began searching for him. He ran toward the pond where they used to gather lotus flowers but found no sign of Mokshith. He checked to see if Mokshith had taken the flowers, but the untouched blooms revealed nothing. He hurried to the spot where Mokshith enjoyed watching the sunrise. When he reached the base of the hill, he saw a figure sitting on top, facing the sun. However, Dhruv recognised it as Mokshith. Slowly, he began climbing the hill to reach him. After some effort, he finally reached the top and found Mokshith sitting on the rock, and the lotus flowers were kept beside him. Dhruv sat behind Mokshith as he silently gazed at the sun, urging Dhruv to join him. A comfortable silence settled between them for a while.

"Dhruv, do you recall how and when you arrived here?" Mokshith asked, gazing at the sun.

"When I was three years old, my father brought me here and said, 'You can play with these kids; I will return in the evening to take you home.' However, he never came back for me."

"Have you ever considered why he left you here?"

"No, he must have a reason for that. I cried for him for a year, and then, slowly, I forgot him. One day, you will also forget her, my friend. Let time heal your pain," said Dhruv, placing his hand on Mokshith's shoulder with more concern.

"Dhruv, are we meant to be here in this life, or are we simply the result of someone else's actions?" Mokshith asked.

"Mokshith, please don't hurt yourself."

"It's getting late. We should go now; the congregation is about to start," Mokshith said as he walked away.

However, Dhruv stayed in a contemplative state as he watched the sun.

The congregation began, and the Enlightened One started his speech.

The Enlightened One: "Love brings joy to some and sorrow to others. It is the essence of human existence; love fuels the world. This universe is constructed from Love and intended for Love. A person in love immerses themselves, while someone devoid of love remains isolated. Those who discover life within themselves transform into love, sharing their boundless ocean of affection with all."

For the first time, Dhruv chose not to heed the Enlightened One's words. Instead, his gaze was fixed on Mokshith, who was mentally absent; his heart belonged to Sreevalli. Every day, the distance between Dhruv and Mokshith grew. Weeks passed without a word exchanged between them. Mokshith rose early to gather flowers, confiding his anguish to the rising sun and participated in the congregation with minimal interaction. Dhruv felt genuinely alone in Mokshith's presence. Nevertheless, Dhruv patiently waited for his friend to return with healed wounds.

Chapter 9

A Permanent Solution

One day, while walking, Dhruv looked up at the sky but saw nothing—only a vast void. He felt strange, as if he were in an unknown world. Suddenly, he felt something wet on his legs and realised he was standing in a river with black water. Thirsty, he was about to take a handful of water when he suddenly heard Mokshith whispering from behind. He turned to see where Mokshith was. Dhruv noticed a figure sitting on a branch of a large banyan tree, though the person was not distinctly visible.

Then, the figure began to speak."My friend, why are you more concerned about my worries? Why are you suffering with my sufferings?

I know our sufferings are the same. We need to find a solution—a permanent solution." The man sitting on the branch raised his hands and shouted, "A permanent solution! Find a solution before my problem becomes yours."

Again, he raised his hands, laughing and shouting, "A permanent solution! A permanent solution!"

Dhruv was sleeping, his eyes rotating rapidly as he listened. "A permanent solution" echoed in his ears. He slowly opened his eyes to see Mokshith sleeping on the other side of the flowing water. Dhruv couldn't fathom why he had such a terrible dream. He observed Mokshith standing and walking toward the pond. After bathing and gathering lotus flowers from the pond, Mokshith hurried to the hilltop to greet the sun, with Dhruv trailing behind. As he followed Mokshith, Dhruv recalled his dream once more. While thinking about that dream, Dhruv lost sight of Mokshith, who moved far beyond his view. After reaching the base of the hill, Dhruv saw Mokshith sitting on a rock. Finally grasping the essence of his dream, he climbed to the top of the hill and noticed Mokshith sitting quietly, sharing his pain with his beloved, the sun. Dhruv stood behind him and said, "Mokshith, come with me now."

Mokshith didn't question him and started to follow him.

They ventured into a dense forest that Mokshith had never explored before. The entire forest lay on a mountain, and the only secure route was a narrow path. A single misstep could lead to a steep valley below. They crossed the precarious path and reached a flat area deep within the forest. Dhruv suddenly stopped walking and showed little interest in continuing.

"Why did we come here?" Mokshith asked.

"To find a solution," Dhruv replied.

"What solution?"

Dhruv pointed forward.

"There, you will discover the answer to your suffering. Go now, Mokshith. Step out of your pain."

Confused, Mokshith walked toward the place Dhruv had pointed out. After going a distance, he turned back to look at Dhruv but found that Dhruv was no longer there. Mokshith felt confused and continued walking forward. Finally, he reached a place surrounded by tall trees. He stood between them. He looked up and witnessed those towering trees. It seemed there was no air in that place because not a single leaf on those trees was moving. As he observed them, the leaves suddenly began to fall one by one as if they had previously decided to do so. Mokshith was shocked by that sudden occurrence. While he was engrossed in watching the falling leaves, he suddenly heard rapid footsteps approaching him quickly. Turning to his right, he saw a figure dressed in red clothing, his face concealed, wielding a long stick with sharp thorns. The masked person was rushing toward Mokshith aggressively. Realising he was about to be attacked, Mokshith tried to escape by shouting, "Dhruv, Dhruv."

Dhruv sat quietly under the fig tree, listening to Mokshith calling for him. While running, Mokshith was targeted by a masked assailant who threw a small rope with heavy metal balls at each end, typically used to restrain an animal by its legs. The rope caught and knotted around Mokshith's legs, causing him to fall as the heavy metal balls bound his limbs. The masked man relaxed, knowing Mokshith couldn't get up and escape. Mokshith crawled on the ground, shouting "Dhruv" repeatedly in fear. The masked man approached Mokshith and began striking him with a heavy thorn stick. Mokshith screamed in pain, pleading, "Dhruv, help me, please." But Dhruv didn't move an inch from that spot. The masked figure continued to beat Mokshith mercilessly. Mokshith was bleeding and shouting helplessly for help. Dhruv closed his ears and eyes, feeling tense. Eventually, the sounds of Mokshith's cries faded. Dhruv slowly uncovered his ears, realising that Mokshith was no longer present. Total silence enveloped the area. Dhruv felt bewildered by the abrupt turn of events and questioned what he had done. He immediately rose and started moving away from there. While he was walking, memories of Mokshith flooded his mind. Those memories did not arrive alone; they carried guilt with them. Dhruv found himself unable to move forward. The guilt associated with Mokshith's memories held him back. He sank to his knees and began to cry uncontrollably, shouting with profound remorse. Then, he ultimately decided that he could no longer live with his mistake. He stopped crying, closed his eyes, took a long, deep breath, and made the choice to end his life. Rising, he found a hilltop overlooking the waterfall. He stood at the edge, knowing that anyone who jumped from there would likely be shattered upon hitting the sharp, jagged rocks below. Nature seemed designed for those wishing to end their guilt-ridden lives. Dhruv peered into the valley's depths, closed his eyes, visualised Mokshith's face, and jumped from the precipice.

Just then, Dhruv suddenly awoke from his sleep, his face drenched in sweat, and glanced at Mokshith, who was still sleeping. He took a deep breath and began to analyze his dream. In this dream, he found himself lying next to Mokshith, envisioning someone sitting on a branch, shouting, "A permanent solution." After the vision faded, he stood up and took Mokshith to a place he had already planned to end his friend's life. Dhruv realized that the dream had occurred within another dream. He knew that even in his dreams, he could not harm Mokshith. He watched as Mokshith got up and walked toward the pond to collect lotus flowers. Dhruv didn't follow him; instead, he remained seated, deeply contemplating his dream within a dream.

When Dhruv attended the congregation, he noticed Mokshith sitting in the crowd. For the second time, Dhruv was not listening to the teachings of the enlightened one. The entire day was difficult for him, but that didn't mean the coming night would be any better. When that night arrived, it became the longest night for Dhruv. So many thoughts raced through his mind. A normal person may not even consider their actions during the day, but for a monk, even a dream holds significant weight. Dhruv was preoccupied with analysing the cause of those dreams. He worried about what led to such dreadful nightmares and thought perhaps his feelings of insecurity and fear of losing Mokshith contributed to them. Maybe he no longer wanted to lose Mokshith. Many doubts arose in his mind. Finally, that night helped him shed those thoughts and drift into a deep sleep as calmness descended after great turmoil.

Chapter 10

Searching For Him Is Futile

Early in the morning, Dhruv had just awoken from a deep sleep and gazed at the sky. It was calm, and birds bathed nearby where water flowed over the rocks. Dhruv turned his head to look for Mokshith, but he was not there. Realizing he had overslept slightly, Dhruv thought Mokshith might have gone to collect lotus flowers. After getting up, he made his way to the pond. Upon arriving, he could not find Mokshith. Dhruv then reached the starting point of the hill climb and looked at the rock where Mokshith usually sat; however, he was also absent from there. Dhruv deduced that Mokshith had gone to attend the congregation. He was determined not to miss the Enlightened One's preaching this time. When he arrived at the congregation, Dhruv still couldn't find Mokshith. He attended the congregation and stood in line for food after it concluded. Though still in line, he continued to search for Mokshith.

While Dhruv was still looking, a disciple approached him.

"Don't waste your energy searching for your friend. He isn't here anymore; he has escaped with the gold," said the disciple.

Dhruv didn't understand what the disciple had said for a moment and was in shock.

"You are no longer needed by him. He has flown away from you. Now you are alone," said the disciple.

Dhruv couldn't believe it. He firmly believed that Mokshith would never leave him alone. Dhruv left that place and searched the entire hill for him. He went to the pond to check if he was there. He knew Mokshith wouldn't be there but didn't want to take any chances. He kept running, revisiting the places he had already checked until he grew tired. Finally, he found himself in a situation where searching for Mokshith was futile because he had left the hill. He sat on a rock where Mokshith used to sit among the lotus flowers. He lay back and looked at the sky, his eyes filled with tears. Dhruv cried out in frustration. Nobody cared about his cries, and he felt that nobody was going to care for him. He closed his eyes, and there was no light at all—just complete darkness.

Chapter 11

The Old Man

With his eyes closed, Anvesh stood in darkness, listening to his breathing as he waited for the sound of the stream. Upon hearing the stream ahead, he opened his eyes and noticed his footprints glowing in the dim light. Just as he was about to take a step forward, he saw bamboo trees on both sides of the path, adorned with torn white cloth hanging from their branches. As he continued walking, a bright light appeared at the end of the path, revealing what seemed to be an open door to brilliance. Drawn to that luminous glow, he pressed on. In front of him lay nothing but bright light, suggesting that anyone who entered would be completely enveloped by that brilliance. Anvesh began to worry: Should he step into the absolute brightness and emerge forever or remain in darkness indefinitely? Fear consumed him, as there was no middle ground to navigate. He had to choose an extreme path, either toward light or dark. Ultimately, however, he felt that standing still was the safest option. So, he closed his eyes and stood motionless. The footsteps grew closer behind him, and he felt someone pushing him toward the bright light. It seemed the unseen figure was forcefully propelling him into that radiant glow. Panicking, he began to shout. Ultimately, he was thrust into the light, as if being born from the safety of the womb into the outside world. He cried out in pain as he fell into a large thorn bush.

"Help me! Help me!" he shouted with pain.

An ancient, harsh voice laughed before the bush. Laughter and cries of pain vie for dominance, each striving to overpower the other with their sounds.

"Hey, who is this? Please help me!" he shouted in pain.

"Finally, you tumbled into the bush," said a familiar voice with a teasing laugh.

An old man stood in front of the bush, laughing and talking. However, Anvesh couldn't see him because he was completely hidden by thorn bushes.

"Hey, who are you? Did you push me into this?"

"Yes, I pushed you into this."

"Why did you push me?"

"Because you're an idiot, I pushed you into this bush," the old man chuckled.

"Who are you?"

"It doesn't matter who I am. Now, come out from there immediately. Otherwise, you will lose yourself," said the old man, laughing.

"These thorns dig into my skin. I can no longer withstand this pain. Please release me now. Please assist me."

"I wanted to help you, so I pushed you into that bush. Now, you are asking me not to help you. No, I won't do that. I am here to help you."

"These thorns are becoming aggressive now and are starting to tear at my skin. Let me out before my whole body is covered in wounds and scars," screamed Anvesh in pain.

"You should come out on your own. Let those thorns rip your body and clothes. Endure that pain, you fool. Overcome that pain. Leave your old, tattered pieces behind and emerge as a new version of yourself. Come, you fool," shouted the old man.

"No, the more I move, the more these thorns rip me off. I can't endure this pain," cried Anvesh.

"Endure it. Endure it. If you endure it now, you will find bliss later," said the old man.

"I am begging you, please let me out," he pleaded.

"You aren't worth it at all. I wanted to help you, but you didn't want my help. You are such a useless man," said the old man, disappointed.

Finally, the old man handed him a long stick to hold. The stick's sharp thorns made Anvesh's hands start to bleed as he held it.

"Pain is the only way to get out of here," the old man laughed gently.

The light hit his face, allowing Anvesh to see him clearly. The old man's face was rugged, his hair was unkempt, and his golden skin and hands were as tough as those of a young man who works all day. He appeared truly ancient as if he had existed for many generations. The old man pulled him with a stick. As he emerged from the bush, this place felt strange to him. His clothes were torn, reminiscent of the moments spent under a tree, where sunlight filters through the leaves, creating patches of light around them. He looked at his bleeding hand, but suddenly, the blood vanished. The blood marks on his hand transformed into a wound as if he had been injured long ago.

"Why did you push me into that bush?" he asked the old man, who was not looking at him.

The old man walked away silently without answering. Anvesh began to follow him, taking in his surroundings as he went. He had never encountered such a world in his life. Everything he saw was black, dry, and pale. The land and trees were black, stripped of any fruit or leaves. The trees stood bare, and his entire environment felt lifeless to him. There was no room for hope in that place; it seemed strange to him. He noticed that the old man's clothes were black, resembling a monk's attire, covering his entire body with a single piece of cloth. Curiously, Anvesh looked at himself, shocked to realise he was wearing a torn black dress. He had always donned white clothes; until he was pushed out of that bright light, he had never worn anything but white.

"Hey, mister, where are you going now?" Anvesh asked the old man.

"I can go anywhere I want, but I'm not sure where you are heading," the old man replied.

"I'm confused about this place. Why does it feel so strange to me? I've never experienced anything like it in my life," Anvesh said.

The old man walked over and stood under a tree, and Anvesh followed him.

"Hey, old man, when did you come to this place?" Anvesh asked curiously.

"I don't know. Maybe it was fifty years ago or just yesterday; I can't say for certain when I arrived here."

"How strange. You must have noticed the seasons when you visited this place. There must be a season, and it must follow the time."

The old man laughed and said, "There is no such thing as 'time' in this place. Here, you can't see the leaves falling, the sun rising, or even the moon and rain."

"How is that possible? Look at yourself. You're an old man; you must have been young when you arrived here."

The old man chuckled and asked, "How long has it been since you last saw yourself?"

"When I lost my way, I lost everything. My dream was to be the best student to the enlightened one, and in that school, I wanted to discover myself. But since I lost my way, I became nothing. Now, I don't even recognise my own reflection. I've completely forgotten my face and the image of it in my mind. Now I understand that this pale and dry place reflects who I am," Anvesh said sadly.

The old man remained silent.

"Okay, let's move on from my topic. You mentioned there's no time here. How is that possible? No one can escape the circle of Time," Anvesh said.

The old man smiled gently and explained, "Time exists when you move from one point to another. If this place and I are separate, then there is a place for Time. But what if this place and I are the same? What significance does Time hold here?"

The old man began to walk away, but Anvesh remained, contemplating what he had just heard. He looked at the old man walking farther away, his figure starting to resemble a bright light.

Anvesh shouted, "Have you ever felt that you wasted your valuable time alone?"

"No. When I first arrived at this place, I regretted spending my time alone and sought companionship. Later, I realised that giving others my valuable time was an absolute waste. You will never get bored when you are full with yourself."

Anvesh continued to follow him, traversing numerous forests, rivers, and grasslands. They only paused to eat and sleep; otherwise, they kept moving forward.

Chapter 12

Stream

After months of navigating the rugged terrain, Anvesh felt completely drained. The burden of exhaustion settled heavily on his shoulders as he paused, his breath coming in ragged gasps.

"My friend, I am exhausted. I can't continue this journey anymore. I am too tired to continue my journey without knowing my destination."

Anvesh found a round-shaped rock beside where he was and sat on that rock.

The old man stood at the end of the road. His posture was relaxed as he gazed down the winding path, with the sun casting long shadows behind him.

"This is exactly where you wanted to be," the old man replied, his voice calm and steady though tinged with authority.

Anvesh looked up at him, curious.

"Do you mean… is this my destination?"

"Yes, it's your destination," the old man confirmed.

Anvesh laughed, but it was a hollow sound devoid of joy. The hope of ever arriving at the place he truly wished to be had evaporated.

"Is this truly my destination? There is no further trail, no alternate path, just these vast mountains encircling us. I believe you misunderstood me; I do not wish to reach this place. You don't understand where I truly want to go."

The old man turned slightly, casting a sidelong glance at him, and said, "I know. You want to find yourself. That's why you left your pregnant wife and began your quest long ago. I know everything about you. I'm the one who understands you better than you understand yourself. No one else knows you as I do, my friend."

A shiver coursed through Anvesh, a mix of shock and fear stirring within him. "Hey, who are you?" he demanded, urgency creeping into his voice.

"It doesn't matter who I am. It's not about how well I know you; it's about how much you want to understand yourself," the old man replied.

In a heartbeat, Anvesh heard the loud stream. He quickly covered his ears while the old man stood still, calm as if nothing had affected him.

"What is that sound? Why does it keep on following me?" asked Anvesh.

"Stream," the old man replied.

"What can I get from that stream, anyway?"

"It's you."

"What?"

"Yes, the stream will unveil your true existence."

"You mean, is that why the sound of the stream is following me?"

"No. That stream isn't following you. It made you follow it. That stream has brought you here for yourself."

Anvesh expels his breath with a heavy laugh filled with disappointment.

"I left my wife and the happiness we shared, abandoning everything to embark on my journey of self-discovery. Yet, all I have achieved is an unbearable loneliness. What more does this stream expect me to lose for me to truly know myself?" Anvesh asked the old man, frustrated and pale.

"Yourself. Lose yourself," the old man replied.

Anvesh laughed wearily, and his spirit was weighed down by hopelessness. "I believed I would find my life's purpose during this journey and return to my wife to live happily ever after. But now, I realise that will never happen. During my journey, I encountered a tree and teased it for standing still in one place throughout its life. Now, I understand that the tree endured rain, wind, and harsh sunlight without water, silently bearing its pain. Through all the seasons and challenges, it remained quiet. Yet, I am someone who believes that movement is life. I sit here like a dry, pale tree, listening to your words that are trying to give me hope. My friend, please don't waste your time trying to give hope to this dead tree."

"Being alone is the most painful experience a person can endure. Embrace that unbearable pain, and you will discover yourself within it. You have been overly concerned about yourself. You cannot achieve anything beyond your current limited version. How can you become a new version of yourself while clinging to your limitations? Let go of the old version. Combine your older version with your ego and let them drift away together, far from you, forever. You must lose yourself to truly find yourself. Go now," the old man instructed firmly.

Anvesh turned his head in search of the stream, but all he saw were immense mountains. There was no stream in sight, and he couldn't hear the stream sound. Tired of searching, he closed his eyes and remained quiet for a moment. The old man also shut his eyes. Anvesh heard the rushing sound of a stream to his left. Instantly, he opened his eyes and glanced in that direction. He spotted a massive mountain with patches of golden grass, so large that he couldn't see its peak. The sound of the stream was coming from behind that mountain. He looked around and saw only the mountain to his left remaining; all the mountains surrounding him had vanished.

The old man said, "Now you can go, my friend."

Anvesh stood up and began climbing the mountain.

However, after fifteen steps, he felt an overwhelming force pulling him back. Confused, he struggled to take even a single step forward as if something heavy were inside him. Turning back, he found the old man sitting on the rock where Anvesh had once sat.

"Friend, I don't know what is happening to me. When I try to move forward, my heart aches. Please help me climb this mountain!" Anvesh shouted.

The old man sat in silence, not responding.

"Oh! I forgot. I know you won't help me," Anvesh said, laughing in despair.

"I cannot help you, my friend. I have fulfilled my duty by bringing you here. Beyond that, I am unable to assist you. I sincerely apologise," the old man replied, filled with guilt and sorrow, tears brimming in his eyes.

Anvesh drained of energy, sat down, breathing heavily, and closed his eyes.

"This stream is nothing but your thoughts and memories. When your thoughts and memories peak, the intensity of the stream rises dramatically. At that moment, you cannot take a single step forward. Take a rest and allow the intensity to subside before you start your climb."

With his eyes closed, Anvesh listened to a voice speaking to him. Although the old man remained silent, the words appeared to echo Anvesh's thoughts. He opened his eyes and looked at the old man, who slowly opened his eyes and regarded him with a mysterious smile. Then the voice resumed, even though the old man did not utter a word.

"Don't worry about reaching the mountain's peak or how long the journey will take. The best time to climb is at sunset. Climbing is not advisable at sunrise because the stream is at its highest level. Take this opportunity to rest and wait for sunset. Remember two key points: never attempt to climb when the stream is at its highest level, and don't start climbing while the sun is shining."

Anvesh looked at the old man, who smiled back.

"Are you suggesting that I remain calm for half the day and then start climbing at night?" Anvesh asked.

"No. Here, the sun rises and sets according to your memories and thoughts. Everything here, including the stream, mirrors your memories and thoughts."

As sunrise approached, Anvesh lay on the rock, gazing at the sky.

"Friend, why are people so selfish? They destroy the very nature from which they came for their own gain. Humans are often self-centred. I am also one of them, as I have come this far only for myself. Everything I sought to do was solely for my own happiness and wisdom to become a better version of myself. But is it possible to love others more than we love ourselves? Does such a thing truly exist in this nature?" Anvesh asked.

However, the old man remained silent. As the sun set, Anvesh, along with the old man, began to climb the mountain.

Anvesh glanced at him and asked, "Have you ever loved someone more than you love yourself?"

He waited for a response, but the old man remained silent. All of a sudden, the stream peaked, causing Anvesh and the old man to cover their ears and sit on the golden, grass-covered ground. Just as Anvesh was about to close his eyes, the stream calmed down, and they resumed their climb. After stepping three feet ahead, the stream surged unexpectedly. Anvesh was pushed back hard, losing his balance and nearly falling. The old man caught him just in time, preventing a disastrous fall.

"Oh, thank you, my friend! You finally helped me!" Anvesh laughed.

"Let's keep climbing," said the old man, and they continued.

Whenever the stream peaked, they took a break, and when it calmed, Anvesh stood up to climb again. They followed the sun as it rose and set, reaching the mountain's halfway point. Suddenly, the sun shone brightly, and Anvesh decided to wait for the sunset. However, it took a long time to set. While resting on a rock, Anvesh turned to ask the old man something but realised he was no longer beside him. Confused, Anvesh looked around and saw the old man sitting on the rock where he had rested before starting to climb.

"Hey! What's going on? You were with me, and now you're back there? How did you get there so quickly? That's impossible!"

The old man remained silent once more.

As the stream peaked, Anvesh covered his ears to block out the overwhelming noise. After a while, it went quiet, and he began climbing again. To his astonishment, the old man appeared beside him.

"Hey, old man, what's going on? I don't understand this mystical occurrence. You're with me as I climb, but you're at the bottom when I take a break. Which of you is real—the one sitting alone on the rock or climbing with me?" Anvesh expressed his confusion.

"Just keep climbing; you'll find out," replied the old man.

Chapter 13

A Lesson From A Flower

Anvesh continued to climb until it was time to sleep. They both lay on the rock, gazing at the stars.

"Friend, I asked you something this morning: Have you ever loved anyone more than you love yourself?" Anvesh inquired of the old man.

"Yes, I loved someone."

"Who was it? Your wife? Your children?"

"Actually, there was a time when I loved a flower."

"What?!" Anvesh marvelled at the old man's response.

"While wandering aimlessly, I began to ponder the purpose of spending time alone when I noticed a tree—the only one adorned with flowers and fruits in that dry, lifeless land. I started resting beneath that tree every day. It provided me with fruits to eat and shelter from the harsh sunlight. Each day, the tree seemed to adorn itself with its flowers and fruits, waiting for my presence. I would sit quietly beneath it, expressing my gratitude, as those fruits and flowers appeared precisely when I needed them, not just in season. Despite its many flowers, one day, I was captivated by a single flower bud. I wanted to protect that bud from the strong wind and fierce sunlight. In my efforts to preserve it, I lost track of my own existence, dedicating myself entirely to its protection. My sole aim was to witness its full bloom one day. Of course, that was my own selfishness. After many days of care, the moment finally arrived. It bloomed fully, more beautiful than the other flowers on the tree because it had blossomed solely for me; I felt a swell of pride and happiness. I would visit just to see that one flower and then leave. As time passed, my focus gradually shifted to another flower. Bit by bit, the bloom that had flourished for me began to fade. One day, it dropped off. I found a fallen, dry, dead flower and felt a deep sadness. It broke my heart. From that point on, I stopped visiting the tree for months. But then, one day, I decided to return and discovered a flower bud where the once cherished bloom had been. From that time, I resolved to protect the bud without any expectations, fully aware that it would eventually fall. So what's the use of worrying? I realised one thing when I began to give love and care without expecting anything in return: my feelings never changed when they blossomed or when they fell. My love and care remained the same. When we love someone with expectations, we set ourselves up for hurt if our desires go unfulfilled. That isn't true love. However, when our love is given freely, without expectation, it becomes pure."

Anvesh found the old man sitting on a rock, and he himself sat on the ground below the old man, resembling an eager student listening to his master.

"When love is pure, the giver and the receiver become one. The love around us, just like the love within us, is interconnected," said the old man.

Anvesh noticed the old man pointing his finger at the sky. Upon seeing him, he closed his eyes and smiled, and tears of joy welled up, signifying the profound happiness that accompanied wisdom.

Anvesh and the old man lay on the rock on that mountain, opened their eyes, turned toward each other, exchanged glances, and smiled with the joy of wisdom within them. Then they gazed down the mountain and saw the old man sitting on the rock, pointing his finger to the sky, while Anvesh sat on the ground as a student. With his eyes closed, Anvesh embraced the wisdom shared. A sense of peace washed over him, soothing his inner turmoil.

Anvesh realised that he was neither at the starting point of the mountain climb, sitting on the ground listening to the old man, nor on the mountain itself, watching them from afar. He understood that he was observing both but was uncertain about his actual physical existence. He had just embraced the joy of wisdom and recognised that the stream was calm. Eagerly, he sprang to his feet, determined to climb as high as possible up the mountain before the stream surged back to its peak.

Together, they ascended more than halfway, pausing once again as the stream reached its highest point.

"Now, even I cannot find rest while sitting here. Yet, I can sense a heaviness pressing down on me. Are my thoughts affecting me?" Anvesh asked the old man, puzzled.

"Yes, we are very close to the stream now," the old man replied.

Anvesh heard the sounds of many creatures. He heard them crying loudly and screaming in great pain.

"Hey, what is that? The animals and birds are making so much noise. Where are they? Why are they shouting like that?"

"They are by the stream now. They aren't shouting; they are crying and grieving," said the old man.

"Why are they crying over there?"

"They are seeking their true selves, just like you."

Anvesh listened intently to the cries of cows, crows, peacocks, foxes, horses, elephants, hyenas, dogs, goats, and other animals and birds. Closing his eyes, he tried to find calm. The stream quieted down. Once more, they began to climb; this time, he was determined not to give up. He focused on shutting out all his thoughts and aimed solely to reach the mountain's summit.

As expected, he finally reached the mountain's peak. There, he spotted a rock resembling the one Mokshith and Dhruv used to sit on while watching the sunrise. He and the old man approached the rock and admired the view. The sight of the vast ocean took aback Anvesh.

"Friend, the ocean is flowing like a vast stream. It appears to have no end; it's an endless, flowing ocean," Anvesh said in disbelief. He observed as animals and birds jumped into the water, only to be quickly thrown back out. "Why do they jump into the ocean if it only rejects them?" he asked the old man.

"They are all desperate to find themselves, and the only answers available are in this stream of ocean. Everything begins and ends with this stream. That's why they keep jumping into the ocean, only to be turned away," the old man explained.

"Why is the ocean rejecting them?"

"Because they are not yet prepared to understand themselves."

"What must we do to gain acceptance from this ocean?" he pressed.

"'Loneliness.' You must enter an unbearable state of loneliness, where the weight of your thoughts and memories cannot touch you. Only then will this stream accept you and reveal your true self," said the old man.

Anvesh closed his eyes, took a deep breath, and opened them before jumping into the ocean. However, just before he leapt into the water, he wanted to hear some advice from the old man, so he turned to look at the man beside him. To his surprise, the old man had suddenly vanished.

Determined, Anvesh stared at the ocean and jumped in.

Total Darkness...

"I am cast into the ocean of love, where there is complete darkness. I don't know where I am headed; I find myself adrift in this ocean. As I swim forward, my clothes rip away piece by piece. This ocean strips me bare. The harder I try to swim, the more my thoughts—manifested as torn fabric—cling to my legs, pulling me down and threatening to drown me. My body becomes wounded, yet I will not stop. I must reach the shoreless shore of this ocean to meet myself, who is waiting for me. I have to swim now. I have to swim now."

The ocean abruptly expelled Anvesh with great force, sending him tumbling far away. He landed in front of an old man sitting on a rock atop a mountain, weeping. As Anvesh fell near the man's legs, he tried to reach out for help but could not. Determined, Anvesh stood up and returned to the rock, climbing and leaping into the ocean once more. Without hesitation, the water threw him out again, even more forcefully this time. When he landed back on the rock, his left knee struck the surface painfully, and he screamed in agony, collapsing in front of the old man. He clutched his knee, rolling in pain and crying out, but the old man continued to look away, seemingly lost in thought. Anvesh felt more hurt by the ocean's rejection than by his injured leg. He desperately wanted to immerse himself in that stream of the ocean. He struggled to his feet, attempting to walk toward the stream, but he could not even stand; his knee was broken. Anvesh had become a cripple, yet he persisted in trying to rise again.

"My friend, please stop. I can't bear to watch you suffer any longer. You've tried so hard to get here, but now you cannot walk. Stop hurting yourself. It's time to turn back and go home," said the old man, his heart heavy with regret. Anvesh looked at the ocean and responded, "Yes, I am crippled, but I am still alive. Allow me to try until my last breath. If death chases me, then I choose to die in that stream. I won't give up until I find my purpose in this life and understand who I truly am." With strong determination, he began to crawl along the ground. Eventually, he reached the top of the rock and jumped back into the ocean.

Total darkness surrounded him as he sank deeper into the abyss.

"My friend, you left everything behind to embark on this journey of self-discovery. But consider this: what if you achieve your goal? What if you return only to find that your wife has married someone else? What if she has forgotten you and is happy in her new life? Would you accept that? Would you truly feel happy for her?" The old man laughed, a sound full of significance.

Once again, Anvesh was taken into complete darkness, going deeper into the dark ocean of love.

Chapter 14

At Last, The Journey Begins

As he gathered lotus flowers from the pond, he noticed his reflection in the water. He had a full beard, and his face appeared pale. Dhruv had never seen himself with such a thick beard before. The sun emerged, casting light on his reflection. Dhruv immediately turned toward the sun, reminiscing about his friend Mokshith. He realised that recalling all his memories with Mokshith was futile. After collecting enough lotus flowers, he moved away from the pond and headed toward the congregation hall. However, as he walked, the memories of Mokshith he had left at the pond returned, accompanied by the scent of the lotus flowers, and began to follow him. Since Mokshith had left, Dhruv had visited the hilltop daily for the past year, hoping against hope to see his friend again. As time passed, however, he convinced himself that Mokshith would never return, and slowly, he stopped making the trek. Yet now, an insistent pull urged him toward that familiar place. Dhruv wanted to try one last time to find Mokshith. He decided that if he couldn't see him on this trip, he wouldn't return to the hill again. He set off on the path to the hill, feeling anything but excited. He glanced up just as he was about to start climbing the hill. When he spotted a figure sitting on the large rock where Mokshith used to rest, Dhruv couldn't believe his eyes. At first, he didn't recognise the shape, but he knew that only Mokshith would be familiar with that spot, making it impossible for anyone else to be there. Dhruv quickly began climbing the hill to see who was sitting there, observing the person basking in the sun on the rock as he ascended. The person sitting on that rock wore luxurious fabric that no ordinary man could afford. He felt a mix of hope and fear as he silently wished it were Mokshith. Dhruv remembered how Mokshith usually sat comfortably, but this individual had a stylish and confident posture that didn't match his memories. Dhruv reached the peak.

After a long wait, he spoke, "Mokshith?"

The person turned around.

Dhruv's breath caught in his throat. It was Mokshith! A wave of emotions washed over Dhruv—shock, joy, and a flood of fond memories surged back as if no time had passed. "Hey, is that really you?" Dhruv asked him, his face showing shock.

Mokshith jumped from the rock, rushed to Dhruv, and hugged him with great affection. "Dhruv, my friend, I missed you so much," he said with genuine excitement.

Dhruv began to cry and hugged Mokshith tightly. "I still can't believe it's really you. Am I dreaming, Mokshith?" he asked, tears streaming down his face.

Mokshith stepped back from his hug, looked at Dhruv, and said, "No, it is not a dream. I am your Mokshith."

With both hands on Mokshith's shoulders, Dhruv exclaimed in disbelief, "I can't believe it! I never expected you to return for me."

Mokshith laughed. "I came back just for you! So, how do I look now? Am I still your Mokshith or someone different?" He struck a pose with his hands on his hips, making Dhruv laugh.

"You look different; you seem so happy, too," Dhruv said, his eyes sparkling.

"Really? How happy do I look?" he asked teasingly.

"You look as joyful as a madman dancing in the rain," Dhruv said with a grin. Immediately, Dhruv dashed down the hill, laughing. He was aware that Mokshith would chase after him. Since childhood, this playful teasing had been a delightful part of their friendship.

"Hey, stop right there! How dare you call me like that?" Mokshith yelled as he chased after Dhruv.

"Catch me if you can!" Dhruv shouted back, laughing as he raced along familiar paths.

They began to revisit the places they had explored together every day. Those locations waited, filled with their memories, eager to welcome them. They walked to the pond adorned with lotus flowers, where they would collect them and bathe together. Mokshith stood by the pond, pretending to search for Dhruv. Dhruv approached from behind, a move that Mokshith sensed. They wanted to recreate their daily activities from the past. Dhruv playfully pushed him into the pond, laughing, and soon jumped in himself, playing together in the water. After that, they visited every place that held significance for them.

Finally, their exhaustion led them to settle in a spot beside the river, surrounded by trees. They lay on the sandy bank, gazing up at the sky, which peeked through the tree cover in patches. Mokshith crossed his hands behind his head and stared at the sky. He then turned to see Dhruv, who had his eyes closed, savouring the tranquillity with a smile on his face. Mokshith felt happy to see Dhruv at peace. He then shifted his gaze back to the sky.

"Now, I am a free bird, flying aimlessly without a concern for its destination in the endless sky," he said, turning to Dhruv, who had closed his eyes in tranquillity. "Dhruv, I have married Sreevalli," Mokshith continued.

When Dhruv heard this, he immediately sat up and gazed at Mokshith in disbelief. "Is what you just said true?"

"Yes, my friend, Sreevalli has now become my wife."

"Hey, how did it happen?"

"Sreevalli, Lakshmi, and I successfully convinced Sreevalli's father, and we put in a great effort to win over her mother. It took quite a while to gain her approval, but ultimately, she accepted me. Now, I am her favourite," said Mokshith peacefully.

"I am genuinely happy for you, Mokshith," Dhruv said sincerely.

"Come with me, Dhruv. I will show you what real happiness is," Mokshith said excitedly. However, when Mokshith looked at Dhruv, his excitement faded. It vanished, and guilt emerged.

"Dhruv, I left you here alone. I didn't even inform you before I left. I simply escaped from you at midnight like a thief. Did you get angry with me? Are you still angry with me?"

Dhruv met Mokshith's gaze, pain evident in his eyes. "After you left, I visited that hilltop daily, hoping to see you again. I clung to the belief that one day, you would be waiting for me there if I kept returning to that rock on the hill. But that day never came. You were always on my mind, and I searched for any sign of you during those visits."

Mokshith kept looking at Dhruv, listening with a heavy heart full of guilt.

"My father promised he would come back for me when he left that place. But you didn't even let me know that you were leaving. You both left me behind."

Mokshith felt a wave of sadness as he imagined Dhruv's loneliness in his absence. "What if I leave you again?" Mokshith asked, fearing that Dhruv might feel upset.

With tears in his eyes, Dhruv held Mokshith's hands and gazed at him. "Please don't say anything like that, Mokshith. I can't endure that pain again. I beg you, stay with me forever. The happiness you're experiencing there isn't permanent. Soon, you'll return to me," said Dhruv, tears streaming down his face.

"Everyone should have their own journey, and I have chosen mine—it has already begun. Now, it's time for you to embark on your own journey, my friend," Mokshith said, expressing deeper concern for Dhruv.

Dhruv angrily released Mokshith's hands and said, "What you have chosen isn't your true journey. At first, you may find happiness and peace, but ultimately, you will discover misery when you reach your destination."

"Dhruv, why should we worry about the destination before even starting our journeys? Look at this flowing river, those trees, those flowers, those mountains, and the sky above. Do you truly believe these were created for us? No, they existed long before our arrival and continue to exist. We're quite new to them. No one can claim to know what the beginning and the end are. Let's go with the flow. It's time for you to start your journey without me. It's time for you to forget me permanently, my friend. Though our paths are different, who knows if one day we will meet at the same destination? Let not worry touch you, my friend; just keep moving," said Mokshith.

Dhruv looked at Mokshith, marvelling at his depth of knowledge, and continued to watch him.

"Dhruv, oh Dhruv."

Dhruv heard someone calling him from behind.
He turned around to see.

"Hey, Dhruv! What are you doing all alone over there? Come on, let's go now. The congregation is about to start," said a disciple dressed in white.

"I am sorry. I dwelled in my memories for a while," said Dhruv. He stood up and began walking toward the disciple. After a few steps, Dhruv glanced back at the spot where he had been with Mokshith, but Mokshith was not there. A sense of peace and calm washed over Dhruv as if he were a seeker who had long lost his way and had finally discovered a path to his destination. Dressed in white, Dhruv, the disciple and member of The Enlightened One's school, left Mokshith's memories in the footprints behind him and walked alongside his fellow disciple.

Chapter 15

Kushaala

"Get up, get up!" A gentle voice calls to Anvesh from afar.

The soft voice gradually increased in volume until it penetrated Anvesh's awareness. Blinking awake, he noticed a young monk, who appeared to be no more than 19, cradling him in his lap. The monk was dressed in vibrant saffron robes that danced in the wind.

"Who are you? Why are you lying by the pond?" the monk asked, curious and concerned.

Initially, Anvesh couldn't respond due to his low energy. Eventually, he recovered and asked, "Who are you?"

"I am Kushaala. I saw you lying by this pond as I passed by."

Anvesh tried to get up but found himself too weak. Kushaala assisted him in sitting up. As Anvesh unintentionally glanced at the pond, he saw an insect that had fallen in and was struggling to get free. The insect's attempts to escape generated ripples, yet it remained unaware that those ripples were thwarting its efforts. Ironically, the creature became ensnared by its own actions. Anvesh studied the insect closely and recognized that he was not so different from it.

"Friend, are you okay?" asked Kushaala.

Anvesh glanced at Kushaala and sensed a familiar recognition.

"You look so exhausted; something seems to be bothering you for sure," Kushaala said.

"Yes, I am exhausted from being alone," Anvesh answered.

"I must reach my destination before sunset. I cannot leave you here in this condition. You should not start your journey alone. Please come with me," Kushaala requested, looking into Anvesh's eyes.

When Anvesh found himself at a loss for words to refuse, he nodded unconsciously, agreeing to accompany him. They began their journey together through lush forests fragrant with pine, expansive fields beneath the open sky, steep mountains, and bright rivers shimmering like silver.

"Kushaala, where are we going now?" Anvesh asked, exhausted from walking.

"We are heading to a village whose name I do not even know. What I do know is to walk in the direction my master instructed me. He said that by sunset, whatever village I reached would be my destination if I kept walking as he directed. My master asked me to stay there until the landlord found his peace. You can take a rest in that village. After you recover yourself, then you can start your journey."

They continued walking, passing through forests, hills, rivers, and lands. While they walked, Anvesh noticed a rounded rock atop a hill covered in lush green grass. He and Kushaala needed to climb that hill to move forward. Anvesh gazed at the rock for a while, captivated by its shine in the rising sunlight. He looked up at the sun and felt that it was missing someone.

Deep in thought, Kushaala noticed him standing before the rounded rock and then realised that Anvesh had not followed. He asked, "Friend, what are you doing? Come, let's go further."

Anvesh resumed following him. They soon came across a pond adorned with lotus flowers. Anvesh silently watched the pond until they moved past it.

As they finally reached the village, the sun sank below the horizon. They stopped at the entrance. While Anvesh wanted to ask who would lead them to the landlord's home, he refrained, knowing what was about to happen. A figure came toward them, holding a lamp and a lone blanket.

"Are you coming from the enlightened one?" the person standing in front of them asked Kushaala.

"Yes, I am coming from the place of the enlightened one," Kushaala replied.

"My name is Raghu, and I serve my landlord. Please allow me to escort you to the landlord's house."

They began to follow Raghu, who was holding a lamp and a blanket. Since it was dark, Raghu lit the lamp.

"Please take this blanket if you feel cold," said Raghu.

"No, thank you. I am used to much harsher cold than this," Kushaala answered.

Anvesh followed them, didn't talk to Kushaala, and silently witnessed them. After reaching their destination, Kushaala and Anvesh entered a room. That room had been arranged for Kushaala to stay in comfortably. However, Anvesh found it impossible to sleep; his mind was a tempest of doubts and confusion, swirling like the currents of the water outside.

The next morning, Anvesh woke up early and noticed Kushaala meditating. He glanced at the door, subconsciously hoping it would open as if expecting someone's arrival. Just as he contemplated this, the landlord walked in through the door.

"I hope you had a pleasant night", said the landlord.

"Indeed, I appreciate your hospitality," Kushaala replied.

Anvesh glanced at the landlord, who ignored him completely, acting as though Anvesh wasn't in the room.

"Now, tell me, what troubles you?" Kushaala asked the landlord.

The landlord approached and sat on the ground in front of Kushaala.

"Master, I possess money, power, a family—everything that I own. Nothing will prevent me from controlling anyone in this village if I desire. Yet, despite having everything, I cannot sleep peacefully. Something weighs on my mind. I live in fear, even though I am always surrounded by those who love me. Please relieve my suffering and help me sleep peacefully," the landlord pleaded.

"There's no need to worry. I'm here to assist you. Don't be afraid; just be patient," Kushaala comforted the landlord.

Anvesh silently witnessed their emotional exchange. As the landlord prepared to exit the room, he paused at the door and asked,

"Master, I heard the news that our enlightened one is no longer with us. I find myself curious: who will be the next enlightened one to take his place? May I know this?"

Kushaala answered with conviction, "Dhruv."

Upon hearing the name "Dhruv," the landlord remained silent, offering only a polite smile before exiting the room. After stepping out, he leaned against the wall, closing his eyes to succumb to his thoughts.

"Your purpose in visiting that village has been fulfilled. Just as I anticipated, you have arrived here from the village. A teacher cannot instruct every student in the same way; understanding each student's mindset is essential for effective teaching. This is why I encouraged you to make your own decisions. Your friend is more concerned about your journey and wonders whether you are on the right path. Our ultimate goal shapes the route we take. You have chosen your own path, which should bring you contentment. You will need material pleasures for your journey as you step into the material world. Now, I would like to offer you something that may temporarily ease your pain. Take these bags of gold with you. Go now and seek your experiences," said the Enlightened One to Mokshith, who stood listening attentively before him.

With tears in his eyes, Mokshith raised his head to look at the enlightened one. As the Enlightened One spoke, Mokshith accepted the wealth and began his journey toward the village where Sreevalli was. Just as Mokshith was about to cross the hill where he used to reside, he paused, closed his eyes, remembered Dhruv for the last time, and softly murmured, "I am sorry, Dhruv, my friend."

Mokshith, the landlord who had spoken with Kushaala before leaving his room, leaned against the wall, his voice heavy with regret as he murmured, "I apologise, my friend. You're right; I've chosen a path of sorrow. I've let you down as a friend."

With a sorrowful heart, Anvesh walked outside. Upon his exit, he discovered a stunning garden alive with flowers and peacocks. As he stepped in, a peacock flaunted its magnificent tail. Behind the dancing peacock, he noticed someone hiding. Anvesh clapped his hands, startling the peacock, which swiftly took flight. At that moment, he spotted a boy about four years old, looking at him and laughing.

"Mother, come here; look at him," said the boy.

Anvesh was taken aback when he saw the boy's mother, Mayuri, his wife whom he had deserted while she was pregnant, enter the garden. Confused, he gazed at her, tears welling up in his eyes, and started to approach her. He longed to express everything he had held back and missed her profoundly. However, his steps faltered when he noticed a man coming towards them, embracing Mayuri from behind. It dawned on Anvesh that Mayuri had remarried, and the boy was their child. Though initially pained, he gradually felt a sense of happiness for her. Throughout his journey, he believed he had ruined her life by leaving, carrying that guilt with him. Yet, at that moment, he felt liberated from that burden of guilt.

"I was that age when my mother left me at a spiritual school," Kushaala said, standing beside Anvesh, who was astonished to see him there.

"She promised to return for me, but she never did. My father left her, a pregnant wife, to embark on his journey of self-discovery."

When Kushaala said that, Anvesh immediately looked at him and wondered how similar their stories were.

"Look at her, how happy she is now. She has her son and her husband. What's the point of my going there and revealing that I'm her son? What additional happiness can I bring her beyond what she already has?" said Kushaala.

When Anvesh realised who Kushaala was to him, he wanted to hug him tightly and cry. However, he couldn't bear to look at his son because what could he say if his son asked how a person leaves his pregnant wife to embark on a journey of self-discovery?

Rather than looking at his son, he gazed downward and inquired, "Have you ever met your father?"

"No."

"Do you know what he looks like?"

"No. Even if he stands right in front of me, I won't recognise him because I have never seen him, and I don't want to meet him either since he has already chosen his path. Why should I interfere with him? Let him continue on his path."

Anvesh contemplated how challenging it would be to disclose his real identity to Kushaala without evidence. Kushaala then pulled out a golden pendant from his bag.

"This is all I have left. My mother gave it to me before she departed. As a monk, I should not cling to material possessions, but I would like you to have this golden pendant. It may assist you in this material world."

Kushaala handed the pendant to Anvesh.

Anvesh's heart ached when he recognised the pendant. It had been a gift for his wife, symbolising love and unity. Overwhelmed, he watched Kushaala, a young monk, walk away from him. Looking back, he saw them sharing in their happiness. At first, joy filled him for Mayuri, but memories of his own losses crept in: his wife, his son, his youth, and the time he could never reclaim. He felt as if he had lost everything. With a heavy heart, he rose and walked toward the uncertainty ahead beneath the expansive sky. He observed the clouds shifting above him. Bowing his head, he pressed on while noticing his shadow following closely behind. As he continued his solitary journey, Kushaala and Mokshith, the landlord, approached. Both men were dressed in the white robes typical of monks.

"Where are you heading, friend?" Kushaala inquired.

Anvesh, at a loss for words, remained silent. His gaze fixed on Mokshith, and he felt uncertain about what to say.

"We're going to my place, where the school of the enlightened one is. Where do you want to go? Just tell me, and I'll help you find your way," Kushaala suggested.

"I don't know where I should go now," Anvesh replied softly.

"Oh, please, don't begin your journey until you know where to go," said Kushaala.

They left Anvesh behind and continued their journey. Anvesh watched them fade into the distance. However, the clouds wanted to conceal the sun from Anvesh; they transformed shapes and blocked its light. Anvesh noticed his shadow slipping away from him. As he proceeded, he encountered his wife, her child, and her husband. They passed by with smiles that conveyed pity. Others followed: Sreevalli, Lakshmi, Sreevalli's mother, the landlord Dhanvanth, Dhruv, Raghu, and Mokshith, a young monk, all of whom crossed his path with expressions of sympathy.

After walking a short distance, he finally saw the old man who had brought him to the stream, an old companion standing before him. Overwhelmed with emotion, Anvesh could not hold back his tears. He embraced the old man and began to cry.

"I've lost everything and everyone. What have I achieved? You told me the stream would lead me to myself, but it has only taken me to a world of my memories and illusions. What have I achieved? I am alone now," Anvesh cried out in despair.

"You're not alone, my friend. You are surrounded by your memories and illusions. Stop conjuring them in your mind; release them and clear your thoughts—the stream is always there for you. Leave everything behind and go find yourself there," said the old man, revealing himself as Anvesh's older self as he embraced his younger version.

Suddenly, Anvesh, the old man, disappeared. Anvesh looked around in shock for the old man.

"Please, my friend, return. You are all I have left. Don't leave me to face this alone. I can't understand any of this. Come and shed light on it for me. I'm too overwhelmed to grasp what's happening around me."

He shut his eyes and cried out, consumed by grief. The clouds fully engulfed the sun.

Total Darkness…

Chapter 16

In You, I Exist

The stream propelled Anvesh with great force, causing him to tumble before the old man seated on a rock. He had leapt into the stream to find himself, only to discover that it had led him into a realm of memories and illusions. Anvesh slowly raised his head and gazed at the old man on the rock, who stared back at his younger self lying helplessly on the ground. As their glances exchanged, the younger Anvesh suddenly vanished from sight.

Now, Anvesh, the old man with a fractured leg and a stick, remains seated on the rock, dressed in tattered black garments. He struggles to escape his memories and illusions while waiting for the stream to calm. Once the stream stabilises, the old man opens his eyes, rises with the support of his stick, and limps toward the ocean of love on one leg.

"I hear the stream calling me."

"I'm coming for you."

"Can you assist me in finding myself within you?"

"In what era should I find myself with you?"

"I'm en route; please stay calm."

"I'll wait for your permission to enter."

"I was within you. I currently reside in you, and I will remain in you for eternity."

"But I have a question."

"Am I growing older by chasing you, or are you growing older by chasing me?"

"Am I getting older by chasing time, or is time getting older by chasing me?"

"Yes, in you, I exist."

About The Author

Kranthi Kumar is a storyteller who ventures into the depths of human thought, weaving narratives that challenge perceptions and provoke introspection. As a filmmaker, his Telugu feature film PRAVAAHAM (Stream)—inspired by his novella In You, I Exist—has earned six film festival awards, a testament to his ability to translate profound ideas into powerful cinematic experiences.

As an author, Kranthi Kumar explores existence's raw, unspoken truths. In You, I Exist is not just a story but a reflection on human primal instincts, the silent loneliness that shapes our identity, and the endless search for meaning. His work delves into the unseen layers of the mind, inviting readers to question, reflect, and discover themselves through his words.

He continues to push boundaries through film and literature, creating art that lingers long after the last page is turned or the final frame fades.

www.ingramcontent.com/pod-product-compliance
Lightning Source LLC
Chambersburg PA
CBHW062212150726
47991CB00006B/2243